MILES ARTHUR AND THE QUEST FOR THE KING'S SCABBARD

C.E. Zyburo

4/23/16

Greyson,

Always be ready for an
adventure!

C. E. Z

Published by
WEE CREEK PRESS LLC
PO Box 51052
Casper, WY 82605-1052
www.weecreekpress.com

Ebook ISBN: **978-1-942922-08-7**
Print ISBN: **978-1-942922-09-4**
Cover Artist: Molly M. Courtright
Editor: Dave Field
Interior Design: Jim Brown
Printed in the United States of America

DEDICATION/ACKNOWLEDGEMENT

This novel was inspired by John Steinbeck's *The Acts of King Arthur and His Noble Knights*, an unfinished "translation" of Sir Thomas Malory's *Le Morte d'Arthur*. Without these works, as well as the support of Viv, Ted, and Cecilia, Miles Arthur would not exist!

Chapter One

The feeling never gets old. Barely able to inhale, wheezing breaths, lungs on fire. Eyes watery, bloodshot, black. Nose aching, bleeding, probably broken—again. Actually, my whole body feels broken, not just my lungs, eyes, and nose. My ribs ache, my head aches, my legs feel like they won't hold me up much longer. Somehow I stay on my feet for another ten or fifteen seconds, keeping my arms weakly up, my fists at each side of my head feigning a blocking power that I no longer have. And then the inevitable occurs—WHAM! A strong hook that easily powers through my left hand, cutting through my weak defense like a hot knife through butter, followed by a solid jab that strikes me directly on the chin. And I'm falling through the hazy fog that now surrounds me and I see the hard, bloodied floor rushing up to meet me…

And I'm out.

* * * *

"Yeah! Yeah! Is that a new record? How far were we into the third round?"

From my sprawled out position on the floor, I see Kay in a corner of the octagon jumping up and down, both fists raised in the air, celebrating his victory.

"Not quite, Son. He made it twenty-six seconds."

"Shoot!" Kay drops his fists, disappointed that he couldn't knock me out any sooner.

I roll over onto my stomach and spit a mixture of blood and saliva onto the mat. I lift myself up as far as I can manage, which, due to the agonizing pain pervading my entire body, is only onto my hands and knees.

A bunch of familiar, hairy toes come into my still-blurred vision.

"That's right. Bow to your leader!"

"All right, Kay, that's enough. Show some humility."

"Yes, sir," Kay grumbles as he reaches down to me, grabs me under my armpits, and pulls me into a standing but still limp position. I'm hanging like a wet dish towel, like a whipped dog, like a boy who just got beat up by his older, bigger, stronger foster brother.

"Good fight, Miles."

Kay lifts my dangling left arm, forces me to give him a fist bump, then graciously throws my arm over his shoulder and helps me wobble out of the gate in the fence surrounding our personal fighting ring. I need all of his support to make it down the few steps leading me away from that awful cage and into the relative safety and comfort of the "cool down room"—which is basically the opposite of the sauna.

"Here, Miles. Use this."

As soon as I'm seated on a long bench that lines the

wall in the heavily air-conditioned room, Dad shoves a thick, raw steak on my right eye. I guess that one's in worse shape than the left, though I can barely open either of them due to the swelling that's now in full force.

"Thanks," I say, leaning against the wall.

"Here. Drink this." Dad tosses me a full water bottle from the fridge, but because of my impaired vision and reflexes, it hits me right in my already sore stomach.

"Ungh..." I let out an involuntary groan, but quickly try to cover my shame. "Thanks," I say again, taking a sip of the cold water and pouring it refreshingly over my sweat and blood-stained face.

Out of my now semi-clear, not-fully-swollen-shut left eye, I see Dad helping Kay remove the fingerless leather hand coverings and athletic bandages from his wrapped fists, the only "gloves" that are allowed in our mixed martial arts bouts.

"Great fight today, Son."

Dad even squirts some cool water over Kay's injury-free head and into his mouth as he offers his words of encouragement. He tussles Kay's jet black hair in a loving manner and leans over to touch their foreheads together—Dad's manly way of showing affection.

I sigh. I wish I was shown that kind of respect, that kind of fondness, that kind of love. But Kay is Dad's biological son and I'm only a foster child, so I guess I'll take what I can get. I don't act like Kay and Dad and I *definitely* don't look like them, who could be mistaken for brothers, with their dark, wavy hair, muscular builds, and chiseled facial features. My hair is light brown and distressingly straight, I can't seem to put on any weight or build any muscles no matter how much I eat and work out, and I still have what many people—to my further embarrassment—call a "baby face." I don't even share a last name with my foster family, for gosh sakes! They are the Ectors—wealthy, confident, strong, and brave. And me, well, I'm Miles Arthur—an undersized foster child with nowhere else to go.

Chapter Two

"I'm going to my room," I say, able to stand on my own after about ten minutes in the cool down room. Dad and Kay have spent most of this time talking and joking together on the opposite side of the room.

"All right. Dinner's at six. And don't forget to do your homework," Dad says in the middle of loosening up Kay's apparently over-worked muscles.

"I won't."

I begin to limp out of the room, unable to decide which leg to favor as they're both bruised from Kay's relentless kicks.

"Miles," Dad calls.

I pause.

Perhaps he does *have something nice to say to me.*

"Yeah?"

"If you don't follow your strength training schedule, you're never going to get better. You're going to get worked like a soft piece of dough every time."

Guess not.

"I know. I'll try."

I turn and stagger out of the gym.

The sun is blisteringly hot for this time of year as I push open the door to the outside world—and the humidity doesn't help, either. Living on a giant estate—one so big that it even has its own name, Bedgrayne—in the backwoods of Virginia, outside of Alexandria in a little town called Caerleon, certainly is nice, but it doesn't change the weather.

As I open the heavy side door to the mansion I call home, I remember how truly lucky I am. Even though I get beat up all the time, any foster kid would give an arm and a leg, literally, to live where I live. I get good food at every meal, my stomach's never wanting, and I go to the best private school around that I would never have been able to attend without the help of my foster family, the family that's taken care of me for as long as I can remember. I even have my own room, which is bigger than some shacks I know other kids have to live in. And I know, at least I think, that the Ectors love me. Or at least, like me somewhat. Why else would they have kept me around for so long when my real family, whoever they are, didn't?

I trudge through the house to the enormous foyer at the front made entirely of marble and make my way to the spiral staircase at the back of the room, which extends to all of the upper floors including the third, which is where my room is.

"Miles, you okay?"

I hear Mom's voice speak softly from below me as I'm halfway up the stairs.

"Fine, Ma," I sigh, continuing my long walk to solitude.

C.E. Zyburo

"Why don't you take the elevator, Honey?"

"I'm fine, Ma. Thanks," I say without stopping or turning around. I feel weird just *having* an elevator in my house, let alone taking it every time I want to go to my room.

I reach my bedroom at the end of the hall and take a deep breath, happy to be alone. Even on an estate as big as mine, even in a house with so many rooms that I haven't even bothered to count them all, I hardly get any time to myself. There always seems to be someone around.

I peel the now body-temperature steak off of my eye, rip off a small piece, and toss it into my bearded dragon's terrarium.

"Enjoy, Archimedes."

I can't help but smile as he creeps slowly over to his food. He looks so funny. I love the little guy.

I walk to one end of my room, open the French doors, and step out onto my private balcony. The view is beautiful—our sprawling, perfectly manicured lawn with the tennis courts on one side and our personal gym at the other, the manmade pond that Dad has stocked with fish, the shooting range we use with all types of weapons from guns to crossbows. Behind all of this, behind our complex of buildings and other structures used for our personal enjoyment, is our ode to nature—the lawn turns more natural with sloping, large hills starting at great heights in the west and drifting lower and lower into the valley in the east. Even further in the background is our private, lush forest spreading out for acres and acres, over more rolling hills and into the sunset. It's like a fairy tale, living on such a huge estate. If only I didn't have to get beaten

11

up by my foster brother all the time, this place would be paradise. My life would be perfect...

I toss the rest of my eye steak over the balcony and walk back into my room, flopping down on my bed to take a nap. I'm too exhausted to shower first, even though I desperately need one. Besides, Felicia, our live-in maid, changes my sheets and cleans my room every day, so I needn't worry about dirtying my room with sweat or blood. Like I said, not too bad a lifestyle for a foster kid. Nearly paradise. Nearly...

C.E. Zyburo

Chapter Three

"Hey! Look who it is—Farty Artie!"

Oh, no.

"My name is Miles," I say, already knowing that my effort to gain even a tidbit of respect will be futile.

"Aw, c'mon man. Like I don't already know that?"

Spencer Fletchman grabs me from behind and puts me in a head lock before I have time to react. I don't even have time to close my locker before the noogieing begins.

I'm still too weak and sore from my weekend beating to put up much of a fight. Not that I normally would, anyway. I don't fight unless I have to, which is to say, I fight when my Dad and brother make me and never else. Besides, Spencer's nearly the size of Kay, which means much bigger than me, and he has all of his gargantuan football friends to back him up. It doesn't even help that I'm on the football team too because I'm one of the smallest freshmen at Jesuit High and I'm only on the team because Dad made me. Being on the freshman squad doesn't mean a thing to varsity players like Spencer, anyway.

Spencer lets me go with a shove.

"Aw, man, what happened to your face?" he asks, almost sounding genuinely concerned.

"Just training with my brother. As usual," I reply, not having any reason to hide the truth. Pretty much everyone at my school already knows I'm Kay's punching bag. Spencer should, too. Even if they're not the best of friends, Kay and him are on the same football team after all. I guess Spencer is just too stupid to remember. He does usually act like a big, dumb ape.

"Well, with family like that, who needs enemies like me?" He laughs and gives me another nice shove into my locker. I'm so small that I basically fall completely in.

Spencer walks away with a smug grin on his face, a few of his goon buddies chuckling at his coat tails. Even a bully like Spencer Fletchman manages to maintain his own group of friends. Kay, of course, has his own clique as well, just like everyone else. And me? I belong to no clique whatsoever. Lucky me...

I grab the books I was trying to get before my usual Monday harassment ensued and close my locker. The bell rings.

Great.

Now, on top of everything else, I'm going to be late to English class.

I try to sneak into room 404, but Mr. Malory, who is writing the day's lesson on the board, somehow notices me without even looking away from his work.

"See me after class, Mr. Arthur."

"Yes, sir."

I take my seat glumly at the back of the room, which is where I sit in every class all day long.

C.E. Zyburo

"So, class, today we will be starting a new unit on ancient myths and legends," Mr. Malory begins to a few groans and a lot of heads already nodding with boredom.

"Ms. Nentres, will you please share with the class one myth or legend of which you are aware?"

Mr. Malory tends to pick on everyone evenly, which is something I like about him, although everyone else seems to hate it. First up today is Leanie Nentres.

"Um...Santa Claus?" Leanie responds in her sweet voice with utter seriousness. The few kids who are actually paying attention chuckle. I smile, but hold back my laughter out of respect. It's a good thing Leanie's cute.

Mr. Malory scans the room, his bushy, graying hair practically covering his eyes, although I doubt that he can see anyway, what with his old age and thick, circular glasses. He looks like a crazy person. I'm pretty sure he is a little bit crazy.

"Actually, class, Ms. Nentres makes quite a good point, though she may not know it. Many of the things we see around us today are derived from ancient myth and legend, including our beloved Santa Claus. Does anyone else have another real life example? Mr. Williams?"

Jackson sits up abruptly. He'd been dozing, as usual.

"Um... Uh..." he looks around the room for inspiration. Something outside the window catches his eye.

"The knights?" he asks, apparently noticing our high school's sign at the front of the school.

"Is that a question or an answer?" Mr. Malory always makes his students answer questions with statements, not with other questions.

"Oh, um, I mean," Jackson lowers his voice to make his answer seem more confident, "the knights."

"Very good, Mr. Williams. Even our very own educational institution has ties, deep ties, in fact, to the ancient past."

My attention begins to fade as Mr. Malory moves on to more boring topics—something about Norse legends and whatnot. His hour-long period, the same as all the rest, feels like the longest of the day, but eventually it ends and I try to scoot out of his room unnoticed.

"Mr. Arthur..."

Darn! Caught!

I turn around from the doorway and approach Mr. Malory's disheveled desk.

"Yes, sir?"

"You really must work on your punctuality, my boy."

"Yes, sir."

"And may I inquire as to what happened to your right eye?"

"Oh, uh, just sparring with my brother. You know, mixed martial arts." I'm surprised Mr. Malory can tell I have a black eye. I guess it's pretty bad.

"No, I'm afraid I really don't know, but as long as you aren't too hurt, a shiner such as you have earned should be worn with pride as a badge of courage!"

Mr. Malory is grinning awkwardly and has a sly look that I can just make out in his eyes that are peeking out from over his glasses and under his thick tufts of hair.

"I'll try, sir," I reply, not quite sure what to say.

"You know, my boy, I have a feeling you're destined to do great things. Great things, indeed. All hail King Arthur!" He chuckles at his own odd joke that I don't understand. "Be sure to tell me all about your adventures when they do occur."

Mr. Malory looks down at his desk and begins scribbling something on a sheet of paper. He always seems to be writing—always. After a while, he doesn't say anything or look up again. He just keeps writing.

I guess I'm dismissed.

I walk into the hall and begin trudging to History. The bell rings before I'm even halfway there.

Great. Late again.

Chapter Four

Mrs. Crayton is not as on top of things as Mr. Malory, which is really saying something. I successfully sneak into the classroom and into my desk unnoticed. Well, unnoticed by all except Gwen Leodegrance, who's staring at me from across the room. I may think Leanie Nentres is pretty, but there's something extra special about Gwen. I've been in love with her from the first time I saw her in History at the beginning of freshmen year a few weeks ago—but of course, I don't have the courage to say a thing.

Mrs. Crayton drones on for her allotted hour with my class, something about an upcoming Peace Conference that can change the world, while I avoid Gwen's stare and doodle in my notebook. I'm such a coward. I can't even look into the beautiful golden eyes of the girl I love. I can't take in her sweet gaze, her gorgeous golden hair, the amazing aura that she fully embodies. She is the perfect lady—and I can't even look at her.

I haven't gotten up the courage to talk to her yet,

either. Haven't said a single word. I haven't been able to talk to anyone really my entire life. Not comfortably, anyway. I'm too shy. I guess that's why I have no friends...

The bell rings. Time for lunch. I gather my things and continue my effort to go unnoticed as I walk down the hall toward the cafeteria.

I look up and see Gwen at her locker. She's not looking at me now; she's focused on her books or something, so I can actually look at her without embarrassment. Man, she's lovely.

I tell myself that I have to say something, but all I can do is twiddle my thumbs, stalling, as always.

Now's the time. Don't be a wuss.

I take a few steps toward her.

What's the worst that could happen?

I stop.

Wait, what *is* the worst that could happen? She could look at me in disgust. She could ignore me. I could forget what words I want to say to her and make a fool out of myself...

Well, I have to try.

I walk a few more paces in Gwen's direction. She's only a row of lockers away now.

Wait, what am I going to say to her?

I stop again.

I could invite her to the state fair.

Yes! That's perfect! Then it's just a friendly invitation to hang out. Not like a date or anything. No pressure. Perfect!

I lean forward to take another few steps, finally confident enough to actually talk to Gwen.

Out of nowhere, Leanie jumps in front of me. I stumble over my own feet since Leanie caught me mid-step and begin to fall forward. I reach out my hands reflexively, instinctually trying to catch myself, but I accidentally fall into Leanie. Somehow, our bodies align perfectly and our lips meet. We basically kiss for a solid ten seconds before either of us realize what just happened.

I pull back, regaining my balance. I take a few steps back from Leanie, expecting her to yell and scream and slap me across my face.

"Wow, Miles... I didn't know you had it in you! You're so... so... direct!" Leanie smiles and pokes me in my stomach, a little too hard since I'm still sore from Kay's punches.

"Um... I..." I don't know what to say.

"I hear you're a fighter. I knew you were on the football team, but I had *no idea* you were a fighter! That's *soooo* cool!" Leanie leans into me, pressing her body against mine—purposefully this time.

"Yeah, well, I..."

"So, are you going to the fair on Friday?" Leanie looks at me with innocent hazel eyes that remind me a lot of my own.

"Well, yes, actually I..."

"Cool! Me too! Maybe we can go together?"

"Um, well, actually..."

"Miles, you better say yes. You can't just go around kissing girls and then standing them up! That's just not right!" Leanie stamps her foot and looks like she's about to cry. What am I supposed to do?

"Well, I..."

"Miles, if you break my heart, I swear to God!"

Now she really *is* crying! Oh, God, I'm in a panic!

"Um... yes! Don't cry, Leanie! Yes, of course I'll take you to the fair. Just don't cry. Please don't cry."

"Great!" Leanie stops her tears instantaneously. "I'll meet you at the entrance at six. See ya then!"

Leanie gives me a quick peck on the cheek and scoots away. I'm still standing as stiff as a post in shock. Did that really just happen?

I only come out of my daze when I notice Gwen still standing at her locker, only a few feet away, but now she is staring straight at me. Unlike Leanie, she has real tears in her soulful eyes.

She turns around and starts walking quickly away from me.

"Gwen!" I yell and start walking toward her, but she turns her walk into a sprint and runs off down the hall.

I stop in my tracks. I'm too beat up to run, and I doubt if Gwen would talk to me right now, anyway. Great. My first opportunity blown. I wonder if I'll get another.

Chapter Five

I have football practice every day after school—which sucks. Today is no exception. I practice all the time, out in the hot sun and humid, heavy air, but I hardly ever get any actual playing time during our games. In fact, I haven't gotten a single snap all season! I'm the third string quarterback on the freshman team and I was only put there because I have no athletic prowess whatsoever. I'm too small to be a lineman, I can't kick, I'm not fast, I'm not aggressive enough to play defense, and of course, I'm clumsy as all heck. My only skill is that I can take a hit since I get plenty of that at home fighting Kay, so Coach figured quarterback might work out—if I ever learn to throw, that is.

Jesuit High hasn't won the district championship in years, but that doesn't mean we're not competitive. In fact, our varsity team is really, really good this year. We have several all-state seniors, including Kay, who is the starting varsity quarterback. Coach Donovan, the head coach, really believes this is our year to win at districts and go all the way to states, but of course, our cross-town rivals, the St. John High Fighting Irish, will do everything in their power to keep districts away from us. Still, if I were to put money on it, I'd have to bet on Kay to lead the Golden Knights to victory. Losing isn't in his vocabulary.

So here I am at practice after school, fantasizing about all of this future glory that I won't even be a part of, when a football comes sailing out of nowhere and hits me smack in my already severely damaged right eye!

"OWWWW!" I scream, clutching my face with both hands.

"Arthur! Why wasn't your helmet on?" Coach McAllister, the freshman coach, comes running over to me, picks up my helmet off of the ground where it had been sitting next to me, and shoves it into my stomach. I never get any sympathy from anyone. Ever.

"Sorry, Coach. It was just really hot." I put my helmet on and see Coach's death stare with my one good, still working eye.

"Hot? HOT? Arthur, if you think it's hot just lollygagging around, how are you ever going to actually *play* this sport? Hot? Go run ten laps and then tell me it's hot! NOW!"

"Yes, sir!" I don't bother arguing or complaining. That will only make it worse. I begin my first long jog around the field and can hear some other kids laughing behind me.

"Oh, you think it's funny, do ya, boys?"

I can hear Coach yelling even from halfway down the field.

"A bunch a' comedians and not a single halfway decent football player among ya! This freshman team is the sorriest group of filthy little punks I have ever seen in my whole pitiful career! Ten laps for every single one of ya! GO!"

Great. Now the whole team's going to hate me.

In about twenty seconds, I start getting lapped by the rest of the team. I really am not fast at all...

"Thanks a lot, Farty Artie," some of my teammates, if I can even call them that, mutter as they pass me by.

"Sorry," I say, already out of breath as I finish my first lap.

I get slower and slower as I complete my ten laps around our practice field and more and more of the team passes me by, all giving me a dirty look or an angry comment or even a nice shove as they go around. I look over to where the JV and varsity teams are scrimmaging on their separate, well-maintained practice area. I see Coach Donovan smiling and talking to Kay like he's his own son, going over a formation in the playbook. I wonder if I'll ever get that far.

It's unfortunate that there are no cuts for the football team. Everyone makes the team and those who can't hack it cut themselves. I would've quit a long time ago, in fact I wouldn't have even joined the team in the first place, but Dad made me and he would never let me quit. It's all part of my and Kay's "warrior training," as he calls it. That's what all of the sports, mixed martial arts, even fencing and shooting practice is all about. Dad is a former Navy Seal and current Secret Service agent who protects the president. His life has been nothing but action and adventure and he expects nothing less of his sons, even his weak, unhappy, foster son—me.

Coach McAllister has been screaming insults the

whole time and is somehow still not out of breath when we're all finished with our ten laps. Years of practice have made his lungs strong, I guess, which sucks for me because I started running first but just finished last. Impressive, no?

"Arthur, how you even get up in the morning I'll never know. I'm sick to my stomach. *You* make me sick to my stomach! I'm disgusted!" Coach spits right in front of my feet.

He stares at me for a few more seconds, but I'm too exhausted to respond. Eventually, he just walks away.

"Second string, you're up!" Coach yells, then blows his whistle for seemingly no reason at all other than to make more noise.

The second string players line up for drills as first and third get a breather. All of the first stringers look disappointed at having to sit out even for a minute, even for drills. I guess that's why they're the starters. But as for myself, I'm always thankful for a break. I try to stand next to the five other third string backups, but even they are embarrassed by me and move a few steps away to distance themselves from my suckiness—as if it were contagious. This is my life. I'm an outcast, an untouchable, an embarrassment even to benchwarmers.

Chapter Six

The rest of my week leading up to the state fair—and my date with Leanie—is really nothing to speak of. I have school every day—obviously; then football practice after—of course; and then home for my rotating workout schedule—so fun! Only once a month do I have a big fight with Kay in mixed martial arts. My dad isn't so crazy as to not allow a recovery period for our bodies. Well, for *my* body anyway, since I hardly ever even leave so much as a bruise anywhere on Kay. But even during my month of recovery and even after several hours of football practice each day, Dad still has Kay and I training in other ways to make us the warriors he so desires. And of course, Kay beats me in everything we do.

"Always be ready for battle; it can surprise you at any moment and war waits for no man."

That's my dad's motto. Well, the "Ector motto" as he likes to say and even though I'm not officially an Ector, I still have to abide by his rules. He does feed me, clothe me, and provide me a place to live, after all. A very nice place. I do enjoy having a private, Olympic-sized swimming pool and a Jacuzzi big enough to hold the entire Olympic swim team, among all of the other awesome things we have on the estate...

So Mondays are reserved for the gun range, Tuesdays are for archery, Wednesdays are for orienteering—which is competitive map reading, hiking, and obstacle courses, Thursdays we do aquatics, and Fridays are for fencing, which I'm actually kind of good at. Don't ask me how. I still have never beaten Kay formally, but I can hold my own against him, which is more than I can say for any other sport or competition we've ever tried. All of these activities are in addition to our usual mixed martial arts training and weightlifting, which varies from strength to endurance training and ranges from Brazilian Jiu-Jitsu to drunken boxing.

None of this is exciting to me. I'd rather spend my time observing Archimedes or other things in nature, but instead I'm stuck with warrior training—no exceptions. That doesn't mean I can't try to get out of fencing a few hours early to go to the fair, though, which is what I'm about to try and do. Good thing it's our bye week in football otherwise I definitely wouldn't be allowed to go!

"Hey, Dad..." I approach him reluctantly in our gym, already fearing the inevitable answer I'm dreading—no.

"Yes, Miles?" He's busy helping Kay suit up for fencing practice. I, of course, am left to get prepared on my own.

"Um... do you think today I could possibly get out of practice a little early?"

Dad looks at me sternly, his tanned brow furrowing as it does when he's inexplicably perplexed, which is a rarity.

"Miles, you know the rules. One deviation from the training schedule will throw off everything else."

That's my dad. A perfect embodiment of "the rules weren't made to be broken" type of guy.

"But..." what to say? "...I have a date."

Kay and Dad both look at me now, the same look of astonishment on their similar faces.

Kay's shock turns into a smile and he laughs. "Good one, Miles!"

"I'm not kidding. Really! I'm going out with Leanie Nentres."

"How are you going out? You can't even drive!"

Oops. I didn't think about that...

"Well, I'm supposed to meet her at the fair."

"And how are you going to get there?" Kay still can't control his chuckling. He's getting on my nerves.

"I... uh... was hoping someone could give me a ride." I look down at my feet. My cheeks are burning. Now I'm angry *and* embarrassed.

"Well, it doesn't sound like you've really thought this through. In fact, it sounds as if you haven't engaged in any planning at all," Dad says, sounding as strict as a drill sergeant.

Well, that's it then. If there's one thing that Dad hates—more than schedule changes, that is—it's poor planning.

He looks at me, very seriously, and says, "A lack of sound strategic planning will always lead to failure."

Another one of his gems.

"Wait, Dad. I have an idea." Kay stands up, a devious look in his eye. "If Miles can beat me in a duel, you should let him go on his little date. If he can beat me, he must have been training hard and learned at least *some* strategic planning. Shoot, if he can beat me, I'll even drive the little snot to the fair myself!"

I see Kay's evil grin and quickly look to Dad. I have very little hope of defeating Kay, but a little hope is better than none at all, and Dad looks as if he's actually considering Kay's suggestion.

A few tense moments pass. Dad rubs his always clean-shaven chin.

"Well, Kay, you know I'm not a gambling man, but seeing as how this puts Miles' fate in his own hands, the result will ultimately be due to his own preparedness, actions, and decision making ability. Miles, if you accept, I will allow the challenge."

I can't help but grin, even on the *off* chance that something good will actually happen to me, that some luck might *actually* come my way for once.

I stare at Kay as menacingly as possible.

"Challenge accepted."

Chapter Seven

Kay and I are eyeing each other from across the piste, our area of play, ready to duel. The piste we use is not like any other used in modern fencing. Most people, everyone else in fact, fence on a rectangular strip that allows for minimal side-to-side movement and no circling of your opponent whatsoever. Dad didn't like this limitation. He knows that dangers can come from anywhere, that an enemy can attack from any direction, so he designed a large, circular piste, about the same size as our mixed martial arts octagon. And unlike traditional fencing, we can score points by hitting our opponent anywhere, anywhere at all, because "all parts of the body are important." Oh, and Dad allows, he even encourages, corps-à-corps, which is body-to-body contact. Forceful contact is illegal in all fencing competitions that I know of, but of course, Dad is training us to be warriors, so for him, physicality is a necessity.

This may not be an important match for Kay, but to me it means the world—and not just because I have a date with Leanie. In all honesty, I really don't care too much, if at all, about my date. I really just want to go to the fair for two reasons: to get out of my house, which feels like and serves as a luxury prison most of the time, and because Gwen is going to be there. I heard her and her friends talking about it at school. If and how I'm going to approach her, I have no idea. I'll worry about that later. Right now, I have to worry about defeating Kay in this fencing challenge, or everything else won't matter, anyway.

I pick up my foil, my fencing sword, a bit awkwardly. My fencing outfit is stifling and a little too big for me. No surprise there since I'm undersized and don't fit properly into any sporting equipment. Time to put all of these complaints and excuses out of my mind, though. We're about to begin.

"Ready?" Dad asks, then, without waiting for an answer, yells, "Play!"

Kay rushes at me, straight across the circle in a confident attempt to score the first point. But, having gotten used to his brazen assaults, I'm fairly decent at dodging his charges and blows.

As Kay nears, I quickly step to the side when he is only a foot away and his slashing foil simply whizzes past. I remain untouched.

"Kay! Remember your training!" Dad calls out from his referee's judging area that borders the piste. He can't stand Kay's impulsive attacks.

Kay turns around and we begin circling each other—foils out, knees bent, searching for any opening or weakness to exploit. We've been fencing for years now, though almost exclusively with each other because of our altered piste and more aggressive rules, so we each know the other's techniques and moves nearly as good as our own. Someone is simply just going to come out on top, whether by luck, skill, or both.

We parry.

Useless.

A few more seconds of testing each other and Dad yells, "Kay!"

Before anything else comes out of Dad's mouth, I make a move. I'm not usually the first to attack, which is why I'm doing it, and my boldness actually pays off! Kay is distracted by Dad's interrupted instructions and doesn't expect my thrust. I get him right in the center of his non-sword arm!

Dad is as equally shocked as Kay when the light goes off in my favor signaling that I scored a hit, but he plays fair and calls out, "One point, Miles!"

According to our rules, Kay is now not allowed to use his left arm. Not a big loss, since the non-sword arm is hardly used in fencing anyway, but I can't help but smile as Kay and I return to our starting positions for another round. Even without being able to see Kay's facial expression, I can tell he's angry by his heaving chest and shoulders. He's like an enraged gorilla when he's mad—he starts breathing heavily, almost snorting like an animal. His whole body expands as he inhales angrily. He just has to be the alpha male.

"Play!" Dad yells a second time, letting Kay and I know it's time to begin again. Kay is able to control himself this time and sticks to his training, moving around me like a shark ready for a feeding frenzy.

He makes his move with a high thrust. I'm able to

deflect, but Kay is now in his frenzy. He can smell my blood even before it's in the water.

Kay makes the same move again and I defend in the same manner as before, an obvious mistake. Kay ends up right next to me, much too close for comfort. He gives me a fierce shove that, in his rage and with his crazy adrenaline and testosterone flowing, sends me flying through the air. I land on my back with a heavy thud and before I know it Kay's on top of me, ready to land a forceful stroke aimed right at my heart. It would be an instant kill shot, but I am able to defend at the last millisecond, pushing away his blade with my own so that the tip of his foil presses angrily into my left arm instead of my chest.

The light goes off for Kay.

"One point, Kay!" Dad yells happily, but I can see that Kay is less pleased knowing how close he was to winning.

Kay and I return to our starting places, both without the use of our left arms now, but Kay isn't satisfied with being all tied up. He's still raging. His whole being will continue growing with aggression until his bloodlust is quenched with victory.

Not if I can help it.

"Play!" Dad calls out once again. I immediately feint a thrust, thinking Kay would believe in my attack. He laughingly swipes my foil away, reading my move like a book.

I step back, trying to stall in order to form another plan. But Kay's too smart to allow me to do that. Well, maybe not smart, but instinctive. His instincts certainly always seem to kick in at the right time when it comes to physical activity, and right now is no exception.

Kay moves in with full force, aiming low in the hope of catching me off guard. It works, I'm not expecting it, but even I have *some* instincts and I reflexively leap over his blow like a kid jumping rope.

Unfortunately for me, Kay isn't only trained in classical fencing technique, which of course makes him more of a threat. Instead of pulling back to resume his approaching posture as most fencers would after an unsuccessful attack, Kay combines his knowledge of mixed martial arts and continues his swiping motion, rotating completely around as if he were attacking with a 360 spin kick.

Again, not what I was expecting. By the time I realize what's happening, Kay's foil is already coming back around, this time aimed directly at my head.

My only option is to make a quick, awkward block, but my wrist is in such a bad position that Kay's close range, full-force blow knocks my foil out of my hand and sends it soaring out of the ring.

I am now utterly weaponless and utterly hopeless.

Kay laughs and struts around me, deciding just how he wants to make his kill.

"Finish him, Kay!" Dad isn't a fan of showboating.

Kay makes a fake lunge at me, just to taunt me once more, and then moves in for his grand finale. He's obviously going for my head, a move that only someone as cocky as Kay would make. His best option would be to go for my body—such a big, open, defenseless target. But not Kay. He's got to prove he's so much better than me.

As his foil flies through the air in my direction, something in me screams not to give up.

C.E. Zyburo

I'm not a quitter.

At the last moment before Kay shatters my skull, I drop to the ground and kick Kay's legs out from under him. I feel like I'm moving at the speed of light, like something other than my brain is controlling my body. All in one fluid motion, as Kay falls to the ground from my kick, I pounce up onto my feet and elbow Kay's foil-wielding arm directly on his bicep, causing his grip to loosen. Even as he hits the mat, my foot moves to his foil hand and I kick his weapon free. I grab it out of the air and without even thinking jab him in the chest, smack in the middle of his heart.

The light goes off in my favor.

No one says a word.

I have won.

Chapter Eight

For the first time in my life, my whole life, my entire existence that I can remember, I have beaten Kay! I've never even won a game of cards against him, but now, I've defeated him in a duel! I'm the winner! The champion! The victor! And it doesn't even matter how I did it, because the deed is done! I don't remotely understand what happened, how I could've made those lightning-fast moves all at the right time, all at the exact instant I needed to, but I did! And now I get to go to the fair!

Dad and Kay are both speechless as Kay and I get prepared for our big night out. Even I don't know what to say.

Once Kay and I are all spiffed up in some nice but not overly-dressy clothes and practically bathe ourselves in cologne, we're ready to go.

We come downstairs from our separate bedrooms and meet in the foyer, our usual meeting place before going anywhere together. Mom comes out from the living room or kitchen or wherever she happened to be.

"Hey, boys. Where are you off to?"

Without slowing down on our way out the door, Kay calls over his shoulder in a not very happy voice, "The fair. See ya later."

"Okay. Have fun!" she yells back, but we're already through the side door to the armory.

Yes, that's right. This house even has an armory. Kay and I walk through it on the way to our multi-car garage. It's the shortest route, but I also enjoy it because I get to look at all of the ancient to modern weapons the Ector family's collected for generations. Walking from one end of the room to the other is like moving through time. There are ancient weapons like Greek helmets and spears greeting us with their golden brilliance. A few steps later and we're passing into the medieval period with full suits of armor, swords, and shields, all of which look incredibly heavy and nearly impossible to lift, let alone fight with. Then come muskets and bayonets and canons with their explosive power, and after that is the most plentiful assortment of all—the modern-era weapons that Dad's personally collected, which includes everything from Kevlar body armor to all types of revolvers and assault rifles. We do practice with all of these things as part of Dad's extensive and fully inclusive warrior training. I must admit, using all of these weapons, from firing a canon to target practice with an assault rifle, is actually pretty cool. It's incredibly fun and not an experience most kids get to enjoy. Of course, Dad keeps all of the ammunition and live explosives in a vault that only he has access to. Safety first.

Tonight, though, there's no time to stand in awe in front of this vast collection of human ingenuity in destructive power. I have more important things to worry about—like how I'm going to ditch Leanie and make peace with Gwen.

Since Kay is Dad's golden child, he of course has access to any car in the garage. Tonight he's chosen the 1968 Shelby Cobra GT 500KR. I can't complain—it's one of my favorites, too. We'll certainly impress the ladies in this ultra-rare classic. The metallic blue paint with racing stripes, the custom Italian leather interior, and Kay's driving prowess can't fail to impress.

Kay pulls away from our estate slowly and safely, but as soon as he's out of earshot he guns it. We make it to the fairgrounds in record time. Neither of us says a word the whole way. He must be fuming at having lost to me, but I'm not going to apologize, even though I do kind of feel bad that he's so upset about it. Oh well. I know what it's like to lose. Yeah, it sucks, but he'll get over it. I always do.

Kay parks in the jam-packed dirt field serving as the fair parking lot for two weeks out of the year. He hops out of the car, slams his door, and starts walking away. Without turning around he yells at me, "Meet back here at midnight. Don't be late."

"Okay," I say, but Kay doesn't wait for my answer. He's off to find his friends.

I walk to the entrance of the fairgrounds slowly, still trying to formulate a plan, but my thoughts are suddenly interrupted by Leanie running up to me, arms crossed, a scowl on her face.

"You're late," she says angrily.

"Sorry. Had to fight to get here." If only she knew.

"You better make it up to me. Like, win me a big stuffed animal or something."

C.E. Zyburo

"Okay."

She smiles.

"Okay! Let's go!" She locks her arm around mine and we stroll up to the ticket counter.

"I'll have a wristband, please," I tell the guy in the booth.

Leanie scowls at me.

"Oh, sorry. I mean, two wristbands, please." Well, that drains half of my savings right there. Even though I live with an incredibly affluent family, I have almost no money of my own. I only have what I manage to save of birthday money, which is surprisingly little since I don't know any relatives other than my immediate foster family, and they give me a total of fifty bucks each year. Dad says it builds character...

So tonight I brought pretty much all of the money I have and most of it is gone before even setting foot in the place.

The guy in the booth chuckles as he takes my wad of cash. He's visibly dirty and has absolutely no teeth whatsoever. I'm sure I'll be seeing a lot of that tonight. Why do people like the fair again?

Leanie and I strap on our wristbands for "unlimited fun" and walk in. There are lights, rides, and the smell of deep-fried food everywhere.

"My friends are already here, but we don't have to meet up with them yet if you don't want to." Leanie nudges me and looks over my shoulder. I follow her gaze and see a ride called "The Lovers' Den," a version of the classic Tunnel of Love.

"Um...okay," I say.

Leanie pulls me toward the ride. I follow reluctantly.

I really just want to ditch her and find Gwen, but how do I do that politely?

We hop onto a seat that looks like a heart. It begins rolling along the track and takes us into a dark passageway. The only lights are glowing hearts and cupids hanging on the walls and ceiling. The soft music of harps is playing.

Leanie nuzzles my neck with her nose. I don't know what to do, so I just sit. She moves my hand from my lap to hers and whispers, "I don't think this ride is very long, Miles. What do you want to do?"

"Um... I... wow, look at that!" I say, pulling my hand away and pointing to a random pink heart on the wall.

Leanie looks.

"Okay..."

We sit in awkward silence for a few more minutes and just like that the ride is over and we're back out in the open air, brightly lit by floodlights and the flashing, colorful bulbs of carnival rides.

We hop out of the couple's love seat and walk in silence between food stands and rides, no longer arm in arm. Leanie is now texting on her phone non-stop.

"Um... Miles, my friends are over by the Round Up. You probably don't want to do that. It's kind of for little kids, but you know how my friends are. So, anyway, I can meet back up with you later, okay? Okay, bye!" Leanie walks away without ever having looked up from her phone.

Well, that was easier than I thought.

I walk in the opposite direction. Now to find Gwen.

Chapter Nine

I have no luck for at least an hour. I even get on the Ferris Wheel to see if I can spot Gwen from above. Nothin' doin'. But I still enjoy the breeze from high in the air. The fair below looks dazzling with all of the lights and people.

The ride ends and I begin my search on foot once again. Suddenly, I spot her, in line to get some funnel cake with two of her friends. She looks amazing in her pink top and jean skirt. I think I'm in love.

But how can I get her to forgive me for that scene with Leanie earlier this week in school? Well, I've got to try something. Right after she orders her food, I make my move.

"This one's on me," I say to the guy in the food booth, sticking my money through the window before Gwen can object.

"Miles..." Gwen looks shocked just to see me. She takes her food. Her friends are whispering and giggling behind her.

"Where's your date?" she asks as we move away

from the funnel cake stand. She still sounds a bit upset with me.

"Oh, that... I...well, it was really a mistake. I really wanted to come here with you."

"Ha! Then why were you making out in the hall with...*her*?" Gwen asks, not wanting to even say Leanie's name.

"It was an accident! I tripped and it just happened. I swear!"

Gwen looks at me skeptically, but a soft smile spreads over her lips.

"Well, anyway, thanks for the funnel cake."

She turns to go back to her friends, but they have silently disappeared, leaving Gwen and I alone.

"Those little sneaks!" Gwen says as if she is angry, but she's still smiling.

"Hey, do you want to go in the Fun House?" I ask.

"I have to finish my food first."

"Oh, right. Duh." So stupid.

"Would you like some?" Gwen asks.

"Sure," I say.

We sit on a bench across from the Fun House. This is going better than I expected, and the funnel cake is good, too! I wonder what I should do next. Maybe put my arm around her? No, it's too soon. What then?

Our hands touch as we reach for the same piece of funnel cake.

"Oh, sorry," I apologize, pulling my hand away. How embarrassing. I can feel my cheeks turning red. Even more embarrassing!

Gwen giggles. "It's okay. Miles, why are you so shy? You're so silly."

Gwen takes the last piece and pops it into her mouth. She even chews like a perfect lady.

I can't help but stare at her. My gaze is just drawn to her. She notices me staring.

"What?" she asks. "Is there something in my hair?"

"No, no. It's fine. You're fine. I mean, uh... You look good. Very pretty." Ugh. I'm even clumsier with my words than with my body, if that's even possible.

"Thank you." Gwen looks at me with her perfect, golden eyes.

All right, this is it, Miles. Make your move.

But before I can do anything I see Kay over Gwen's shoulder. He's with some of his goon football buddies. He spots Gwen and I on the bench and starts coming toward us. Great. The last thing I need is Kay embarrassing me, especially when things are going so well.

"Um, well, time for the Fun House!" I say quickly, grabbing Gwen's hand and pulling her toward the giant open entrance that resembles a clown's mouth.

"Wait!" Gwen says, scurrying back to the bench to throw away her paper plate. She runs back to me and grabs my hand. "Okay, let's go!"

Luckily, Fun Houses are probably the least popular rides—if you can even call them rides—at fairs, so Gwen and I simply flash our wristbands at the guy guarding the entrance and run in without having to wait in line.

We hurry through a room of mirrors as quickly as we can, which isn't very fast at all because it's hard to tell the difference between a path opening and a mirror.

"Miles, can we slow down a bit?" Gwen asks.

"Um, well..." I look back, but already I see Kay's reflection in one of the mirrors. Darn! He followed us in!

"I just really want to see what's next. I don't like this mirror room. Makes me dizzy."

"Okay," Gwen says, and off we go again at a fast pace.

The next section has skinny punching bag things hanging from the ceiling. I lead the charge and plow through them no problem, Gwen still clinging to my hand behind me. But I know these padded tubes won't slow Kay down any more than they did me, so I continue moving as fast as I can.

Gwen and I make it through a dark room lit only by black lights which make our shirts glow, and another area full of spinning circular floorboards and others that slide back and forth under our feet.

"What, you don't like any of these things, either?" Gwen asks, beginning to sound a little irritated.

"Um..." I look behind me again. No sign of Kay. Ahead of us are three hallways, a perfect time to lose Kay once and for all.

"Let's just choose a path and go. Then we can slow down," I suggest.

"Okay, fine. Which way do you want to go?"

Hmm... which path to choose? Which one wouldn't Kay pick?

Well, he would probably think I'd take the first one because it's the most convenient. But would he know I thought of that and would therefore pick another? Ugh. No time for all of this contemplation. Time to go with my gut!

"The middle!" I say, and we hastily move down the dark hallway.

I can't see a thing for a few steps, so I make my way down the hall by groping along the wall with one hand while Gwen's grip tightens on my other. It's dead quiet and pitch black. Neither of us says a thing. The only sound is our heavy breathing and our soft footsteps as we creep further and further into the dark.

Suddenly, I feel a wall in front of me. No, it's a door. Good. It's not a dead end. I turn the handle and hear a series of clicks that sounds like a dozen or more bolts being unlocked. Gwen and I step across the threshold.

We're outdoors. Weird, because we seem to be behind the Fun House in what looks like the back of the fairgrounds. There's nothing around us—no food vendors or rides, just one piece of equipment that's not even lit up and appears to be broken down. We can't even hear the sounds of the fair. There's nothing but grass and gravel below us, some woods further ahead, and the dark, starry night above.

"Maybe that was an emergency exit," I think out loud.

"Yeah. Let's go back," Gwen suggests.

Bling, bling, bling, bling bling!

The loud noises of what sounds like an arcade game or pinball machine booting up shocks both of us. I nearly jump out of my skin as the apparently broken piece of equipment lights up and starts spewing all sorts of noise. It looks like one of those sledgehammer games where you pound a rubber circle to send a weight shooting up and get a prize based on how high up it goes. The brightly lit sign at the top reads "The Sword in the Stone."

"Welcome! Welcome! Welcome!"

Gwen and I jump again as an old man dressed in some type of old, dirty blue robe held up with some rope tied about his waist appears out of nowhere. He's wearing broken leather shoes that appear to be no more than ancient moccasins and he's using a piece of gnarled wood as a walking stick. He has long, gray hair matching his beard which dangles all the way down to his knees. No, upon closer inspection, even in this dim light provided only by the stars and the sparse, dusty lights on the one carnival game before us, I can tell that his hair really isn't gray at all. The color is actually quite extraordinary. It isn't merely gray, but appears more like the color of silver, like strands of mercury dripping from his head and face that have solidified like thin, intertwining icicles shimmering in the moonlight.

Definitely one of the weirdest looking carnies I've ever seen.

"Oh my! Oh my! Sorry if I frightened you. You have nothing to fear from me, my fine lad and lass! We are merely here for your convenience, yes, and entertainment! Would you like to have your rightful shot?"

The old man motions with his arm at the now fully illuminated game.

"Um...I think we better just head back," Gwen says, tugging at my arm. But for some reason, I can't look away from the game.

"Nonsense, nonsense. No harm in just one attempt, for one attempt is all that one needs," the old man smiles and pulls out a sledgehammer from I don't know where. There is an odd twinkling in his gray eyes, the likes of which I've never seen in anyone else's before.

I'm pulled toward the sledgehammer by some unseen force, reaching out my hand for the shaft.

"Miles!" Gwen yells in a subdued scream, pulling at me again.

The old man pulls the sledgehammer back. "Miles? Miles...an interesting name."

He looks as if he is thinking deeply about something, then cheers up and says, "But not the most noble." He moves again to hand me the sledgehammer. I take it. It's very heavy, but somehow feels just right.

"Miles Arthur! Let's go!" Gwen yells, but then covers her mouth quickly with fear in her eyes, realizing that she just gave away my full name to a crazy old carnie.

The old man's eyes really light up now. In fact, they seem to be magically sparkling. "Miles Arthur, eh? Now that is interesting indeed!"

The old man shuffles me over to the game and positions me directly in front of the rubber piece I'm supposed to hit with full force, which looks just like an old blacksmith's anvil sitting on top of a large block of marble. The back half of the anvil is lodged inside of the tower, and stuck inside the anvil is a miniature sword, which is apparently the piece that will shoot up the tower to determine my prize.

Despite Gwen's continuing protests, I cannot move away from the game. I'm compelled toward it.

I move my body into a solid swinging position, ready to strike.

"Ahem!" the old man coughs and holds out his hand, as if waiting for payment.

"Oh, uh, how much is it?" I ask, pulling my few remaining dollars from my pocket.

"Five dollars."

I only have ten left, but I'm more than willing to part with half of my remaining stash to play this game.

I hand the old man the money and he does some sleight of hand trick to make it seemingly disappear into thin air.

I resume my striking position. I take a few deep breaths in preparation.

Here goes nothin'!

I lift the sledgehammer above my head. Suddenly, it's yanked from my hands. My forward motion continues, though, and I send myself falling onto the anvil and marble block.

"Ugh," I groan and roll from my stomach off of the anvil and onto my back on the not much softer ground. My ribs are sore from the fall. I look up.

Kay.

Chapter Ten

"Haha!" Kay laughs evilly, sledgehammer in hand. His two gorilla friends are laughing behind him.

"What's wrong with you?" Gwen yells at Kay, coming over to help me to my feet.

"Hmm... This must be Kay," the old man muses, stroking the top of his shiny beard.

"How do you know my name?" Kay asks, clearly disturbed that such a creepy old man would know anything about him.

"Oh, I know a great many things. Yes. A great many things."

"Okay, weirdo. Hey, let me take a shot at this thing," Kay says, immediately winding up for a strike at "The Sword in the Stone" game.

But the old man is somehow too fast and even too strong for Kay, stopping the sledgehammer in the middle of Kay's backswing with his walking stick.

"Five dollars," the old man leers at Kay.

"Okay, okay. Jeez." Kay takes out a wad of cash

much thicker than mine was even at the beginning of the night.

"Got change for a twenty?"

The old man snatches the twenty dollar bill from Kay and does the same sleight of hand trick he used on me to make it disappear, but also produces Kay's change in one motion.

Kay looks at the man strangely and takes his money, but says nothing.

He takes the sledgehammer and winds up. His muscles bulge. He hits the anvil with full force—WHAM!—but the sword doesn't move an inch up the tower. It doesn't even shift in the anvil at all. Kay is furious.

"Man, this game is rigged! I want my money back!"

The old man leans calmly on his staff and points to a gold inscription on the marble below the anvil, which none of us had noticed before, that reads "no refunds" in fancy calligraphy.

Kay throws the sledgehammer down. "This is BS! Let's get out of here," he says to his friends. They begin to walk away.

But I'm not satisfied. I haven't had my shot yet. I pick up the sledgehammer. The old man holds out his hand for payment. Ugh. I know there's no use in arguing with this crazy old carnie.

I hand him my money. Well, that's the last of it. Two all-you-can-ride wristbands, a funnel cake, and two carnival games and I'm wiped out. Oh well. I can't back down now.

I lift the sledgehammer and take my three breaths. I lift it over my head and bring it down with all my might directly on the anvil—WHAM!—the little sword comes rocketing out and flies up the shoot in the tower—DING!—it hits the bell at the top.

I win! I win the grand prize! And what's more, I beat Kay again! Twice in one day!

I turn around, all smiles. Gwen is smiling, too. But Kay, near the back of the Fun House with his goon buddies, has hatred all over his face. He comes storming back over to where I am standing and grabs the sledgehammer out of my hands.

"Let me see that!" he yells, hands the old man five bucks, and tries again. Big swing—WHAM!—but the sword doesn't move. Kay stands rigid in angry disbelief.

"Moose! You try!" he says, handing the sledgehammer to his big, offensive lineman friend. Kay pays the old man without looking at him.

Moose waddles over to the game. He makes a big, heaving swing—WHAM!—but the sword stays put.

"Sully!" Kay orders his center to try. Kay pays again, but his gaze remains glued to the sword in the anvil, a death stare that would make any man quiver in fear.

Sully, the biggest guy on the team, a guy who can bench press five times his IQ, takes a huge, arching swing. The hammer slams into the anvil with such force that the ground shakes below our feet—WHAM!—but still, the sword remains in place.

Kay turns to me. "Your turn," he says quietly, and pays my way, an unheard of gesture for him, though I guess he's not really doing this out of kindness.

I take up the sledgehammer, happy to oblige. If I did it once, I can do it again. I perform my routine—sledgehammer back, three breaths, swing, contact—WHAM!—and up goes the sword all the way to the top—DING!

I look at Kay. He still looks enraged, but he turns to me and says calmly, "I don't know what this guy's game is, but watch out. He must have a thing for you." He spits in the old man's direction and without another word walks back to the Fun House, Moose and Sully tagging along like the well-trained animals that they are.

"Not very gentlemanly, but he'll grow out of it." The old man looks away from where Kay has just departed and turns to me. His twinkling eyes are mesmerizing.

"Well, we need not worry about that." The old man's mood changes abruptly. "It is time to celebrate! Well done, my boy! You have done it! I have been waiting a very long time for this!"

The old man runs over to the marble and squats down, staring at it. Nothing happens for a good sixty seconds.

Gwen and I look at each other. She leans over to me and whispers, "He really is crazy. Let's get out of here."

"Okay," I say, but as we try to silently slip away, I notice a change in the marble the old man is still staring at. Some new letters are magically forming in the marble, carved in golden calligraphy. The letters slowly spell out, in brilliant writing,

Whomsoever removes this sword from this stone and anvil is king of all by right of birth.

The old man jumps high into the air, higher than any old man should be able to jump. "Haha!" he laughs and screams as he does an odd jig, lifting his robe to better move his bony legs. "Yes! Yes! Yes! The reign of the Great King has begun again!"

C.E. Zyburo

He looks at me, a look of pure ecstasy all about him. "You, my boy, you, Miles Arthur, you will be a great king yet again!"

"Um, well, that's great and all, but we really have to be going. Curfew, you know!" Gwen grabs my arm and tries pulling me away once more, but I'm still being drawn to the old man and the game.

"What do you mean, I'll be king again?" I ask.

"Why, my boy, have you not yet guessed? You are King Arthur! You pulled the sword from the stone! You are destined by blood to be king of all noble lands and citizens, to have a long and prosperous reign, to rebuild your court at Camelot, and to renew the knights of the table round!"

"But I didn't pull any sword. I played a carnival game. I hit an anvil with a sledgehammer," I argue.

"Pshaw! Semantics, my boy, all semantics! There is more magic in this world than you or even I dare to imagine. Sometimes, objects, just like people, are re-made. Even Excalibur—oh!"

The old man slaps his forehead and goes running behind "The Sword in the Stone." He comes back in a jiffy with a bundle in his arms, some long object wrapped in old, leathery rags.

"How could I forget! Your sword, my Lord." The old man kneels and hands me the bundle, his head bowed.

I take it, not knowing what else to do. The old man springs back up. He chuckles and says, as if to himself, "Your sword, my Lord. Haha! I always liked the way that sounds!"

He looks at me. "Go ahead! Open it! Open it!"

I unwrap the bundle cautiously, not knowing what to

53

expect. Underneath all of the rags is the most beautiful sword I have ever seen.

"Excalibur!" the old man exclaims reverently. "The mightiest of swords! Hold it up! Hold it up!"

I do, and it's magnificent. Perfectly balanced, strong but light. Amazing. Radiant.

"So if that's Excalibur and he's King Arthur, then who are you?" Gwen asks.

The old man and I turn to her, having nearly forgotten her existence in our admiration of Excalibur.

"Why, my dear, have you not yet guessed my identity? I, of course, am Merlin."

Chapter Eleven

"Okay! I think we've heard enough! Seriously, Miles. Let's go. NOW!" Gwen says through clenched teeth.

"My dear, now is not the time to be in haste. We have much too much to discuss. But if you doubt my identity, I would be more than happy to prove myself," Merlin—well, the old man who claims to be Merlin—bows low to Gwen in a display of respect.

Gwen looks at me in disbelief. I just shrug my shoulders and say, "Let him prove it if he wants to."

Gwen looks as if she can't believe what I just said. "Fine. You want to play this crazy game with this crazy old man, be my guest," she says to me, then turning to the old man, "But if you start doing anything *extra* weird, *first* I'm going to take that sword," she points to Excalibur still shining in my hand, "and show you how to really use it, and *then* I'm going to call 911, which I have on speed dial," she takes out her cell phone and keeps it at the ready.

Merlin just smiles. "No need for threats, my dear Gwen."

Gwen lets out a surprised squeak. "You know *my* name, too?"

"Oh, yes. Why, whom else would be at young Arthur's side if not the love of his life and future wife?"

Gwen and I are both shocked by this statement. Gwen tries to brush it off and says, "He came here with someone else, you know. A girl named *Leanie*."

Merlin looks puzzled at first, but then nods. "Ah, I see. Nothing to worry about. She is his half-sister."

Gwen looks at me, more shocked than ever.

"*Miles*, gross! You *kissed* her!"

"*I* didn't know!" I exclaim, as surprised by the revelation as anyone and certainly more embarrassed.

"Of course he didn't know. He didn't know it was her over a thousand years ago when he had worse transgressions and he won't know a thousand years from now. And yet happen it did and happen it will again." Merlin sighs. "But, back to the task at hand! As to my identity, young madam, if knowledge and wisdom are not enough evidence for you, then perhaps a demonstration of conjuring will do the trick!"

And with this Merlin begins moving his old staff in a circular motion in front of himself and mumbling in a deep, low voice some words in an unfamiliar language sounding a bit like Latin. The earth below his staff begins to soften like quicksand and then churn in a slow moving whirlpool.

Gwen and I take a step back. Merlin lifts his staff and the swirling earth follows, creating a small vortex about the height of a man. Merlin takes out a small canvas bag that was concealed somewhere within his robe and casts the sparkling contents, shining like tiny stars, into the miniature whirlwind. An image slowly appears, growing clearer and clearer in the silently circling earth. It is like a scene out of a movie. There are knights in armor in a great stone hall and ladies in colorful dresses. At the head of the hall are two thrones. In one sits a noble king who looks an awful lot like me, except for his age and brown beard. In the other throne sits a beautiful queen, who looks almost exactly like Gwen.

"What is this?" I ask, somehow already knowing the answer.

"This is you, King Arthur and Queen Guinevere, when you ruled England in the fairest of reigns," Merlin replies, and then snaps his fingers unexpectedly and the whole thing vanishes—image, vortex, and all—just disappears as though it had never even existed.

I look over at Gwen. Her phone has fallen out of her hand and is lying in the dirt; her jaw is dropped in shock.

"Do you believe him now?" I ask her. I know I do.

"Um... I...uh..."

"I believe that is answer enough." Merlin comes over to me and smiles, his eyes twinkling with pleasure. "Shall we get down to business?"

"Um, what business?" I ask.

"Come with me and I shall explain everything. Just over there. That is my home." He points with his staff at a little ramshackle dwelling built of sticks, stones, earth, and a bit of canvas that I hadn't noticed until now. Indeed, it's hardly anything worth noticing.

"Um, okay. Come on, Gwen," I say, starting to follow Merlin who is already nearing his home, but Gwen is frozen with astonishment where she had been gawking at Merlin's conjuring exhibition.

"One second," I say to Merlin and walk back over to Gwen.

I whisper in her ear, "Gwen, come with me. I'll keep you safe. I promise. I have this sword and I actually have the training to use it. Come on. I have a feeling this is something you won't want to miss."

Gwen looks at me with trusting yet fearful eyes. "Okay, Miles. I trust you." She picks up her phone and puts it away, then takes my left hand in hers. Excalibur is still glistening in my right. As we walk slowly together, I try to lighten the mood by saying, "I didn't know your real name's Guinevere."

"Shut up," she says, squeezing my hand tightly. "I never let anyone know that. I tell all of my teachers before class every year never to use my real first name."

Huh. Learn something new every day.

We walk up to Merlin at the entrance to his very humble abode.

"Okay, let's go," I say.

"This way to your destiny," Merlin replies, escorting us into his magician's den.

C.E. Zyburo

Chapter Twelve

Merlin's house, if it can even be called that, is just as depressing on the inside as it appeared from the out; walls made of sticks, mud, and canvas with unintentional gaps I can see out of, a small, short, shoddy table but no other furniture, and it is lit only by a few candles laying helter-skelter around the tiny place, most sitting on dirty shelves lined with dusty bottles filled with old-looking powders and liquids.

"The beauty of travelling with a carnival is you never need a fire to keep warm!"

It's true. Carnivals travel around the country following the good weather. You never see a state fair being held in the snow.

Merlin sits on the dirt floor at the little circular table. Gwen and I look at each other, but what can we do? We sit down too, getting our nice clothes dirty in the process.

"So if you're Merlin, a great and famous magician, why do you work at a fair?" I ask.

"Why, I was searching for you, of course."

"What for?"

"Because it is my destiny to serve the true and rightful King. How can I serve the king if I don't even know where he is?" Merlin replies, chuckling.

"Just because my name is Arthur doesn't make me a king. And king of what, anyway? Wasn't King Arthur king of England like a thousand years ago?" I still don't quite believe everything Merlin has been saying, even if he is a real magician and can conjure up images in a dirt vortex.

Merlin sighs. "Have I not explained this already? I suppose you think that carnival game out there is the original sword in the stone and that I am the original Merlin?"

I look at Gwen, perplexed. She offers no explanation and looks equally confused.

"Uh…yeah?" I say.

Merlin slaps himself in the forehead. "Listen carefully, boy. Ahem… I mean…your Highness. As I said before, objects can be and often are remade, such as a plastic bottle being recycled and turned into part of a bench, or old newspapers being shredded and pressed back together to form new paper. And, just like objects, even people can be remade. Not the same process, of course, but it's the same idea.

"That 'Sword in the Stone' game out there was made using the same incantation that was used to bind the original sword in the stone a millennia ago, with the same purpose of identifying the true and rightful heir to the throne. It worked then and it worked again. But though the method be the same, the objects are different and even the people are quite different, though both be the same in

60

spirit. Do you really think I could find you by sitting on my you-know-what, just waiting for you to stumble upon a rock with a piece of metal in it? No, no, no. The world was a much smaller place a thousand years ago, and so I could easily find the King using *that* method. Why, London was the capital of the world back then! Fitting I should find you now near the current capital..." Merlin gets quiet, as if lost in his own thoughts.

"Funny, I always thought New York City was the capital of the world," I reply with a chuckle and nudge Gwen, trying to impress her with my little joke. She and Merlin look at me with annoyance.

"Sorry," I apologize, embarrassed at my own awful attempt at humor.

"As I was saying..." Merlin continues, "Travelling with a carnival has other benefits besides following decent weather around the country. I get my room and board taken care of, a few extra dollars here and there, and Fate has led me to my King! And yes, young sir, you are the king. You are not just a descendant of King Arthur, Gwen here is not just an heir of the fairest queen to have ever lived, you *are* them. You have been reborn!"

"Okay, *Merlin*, if people are reborn, then how does the world's population keep going up? I mean, if we all died just to get reborn, the population would just stay the same," Gwen argues, obviously still doubting Merlin's authenticity.

Merlin looks at her with the same judgmental eyes he'd shown me after my poorly timed joke. "My dear, did I ever say that *all* people are reborn? I dare say I did not! There are many things even I don't fully comprehend, but from what I do understand, as far as my knowledge goes, the universe creates and destroys as necessary, and sometimes, it *recreates*. Everyone has a destiny and some are better fit for certain paths than others."

Merlin smiles like an old, wise teacher. "My young friends, you are destined for greatness. It is a very exciting time. You were not reborn simply for no reason at all. A great change in the world is coming and you are at the heart of it. You and your friends and family. It has been more than a thousand years since we were needed last, but here we are again!"

"What do you mean, 'we'?" I ask.

"Well, you really don't think that I'm a thousand-something years old, do you? I am quite old, it's true, but not quite *that* old! I am Merlin reincarnate, of course. I was born Emanuel Constianos Merlinstein, but I find Merlin to be much more to the point, don't you?"

"Okay, so you're a reincarnated magician, I'm a queen, and he's a king. I guess that's believable enough. How else can you explain all of our weird names and all of us happening to be in the same place at the same time?" Gwen says, apparently justifying Merlin's claims to herself.

"Yes, and you both came to the fair at precisely the right time to meet me—for I am a busy man and am not always attending to *this* little game—you chose the correct passage in the Fun House, and you were willing to play a game with a crazy old man. Or perhaps fate led you here, led you all the way, eh?" Merlin interjects.

Gwen and I look at each other. It does seem a bit too much to be just coincidence.

"So, what are we all doing here?" she asks.

Gwen is apparently coming around to the idea of

being royalty. I must admit, it sounds pretty appealing to me, too.

The sparkle returns to Merlin's eyes. I hadn't noticed when it had gone, but it's obvious when it comes back. It's visible even in this dark rabbit hole.

"Down to business, at last. You always were a strong woman, Guinevere."

"My name's Gwen. Just Gwen."

"Oh, quite right. My apologies. So, down to business. Of course, we are all in for a lifetime of adventures now that we've found each other, but the first thing to do is go on quest! I have already discovered Excalibur for you, clearly," Merlin points to the ancient yet still exceptionally sharp and perfectly maintained sword in my hand, "but I'm afraid the King's Scabbard is yours to recover. Now, what you need to know most..."

Beep! Beep! Beep!

Merlin is interrupted by an annoying beeping sound. Gwen looks at her phone.

"Sorry, phone's dying," she says. "You don't happen to have an outlet...do... you..." her thought fades away as she looks around and remembers where she is—in a little mud hut, discussing matters of much more importance than a dying cell phone. "Sorry," she apologizes, looking down at the ground in shame.

"As I was saying..." Merlin continues, "The thing you need to know most of all is that in two week's time, your foster father, Sir Ector, is going to be killed..."

Chapter Thirteen

"...Sir Ector is going to be killed unless you are able to complete your quest, obtain the King's Scabbard, and get it to your father in time to protect him," Merlin says sullenly yet matter-of-factly.

"What's a scabbard?" Gwen asks.

Phew! I was worried I was the only one who didn't know.

Merlin rubs his brow in frustration. "It's the protective sheath for a sword, my dear, and in this case, it's more valuable than Excalibur itself!"

I look at the magnificent sword in my hand. It looks so powerful, so perfect. "So this is the original Excalibur? This wasn't remade?"

"Of course it's the original!" Merlin exclaims. "Excalibur can never be re-forged. The magic that created it has been lost to the world. But it can be destroyed, so treasure it! The scabbard, however, is the true treasure. Whomsoever holds the King's Scabbard will not bleed from mortal wounds—which is why you *must* get it to Sir Ector!"

My foster father, in danger? Impossible. He's an ex-Navy Seal, a fully trained warrior, a Secret Service agent—oh no! That must be it! Someone must be trying to kill the president!

I look steadily at Merlin, studying him for any secrets that his actions might give away. I don't quite trust him now. I don't trust him at all. Is he threatening my father? Is he threatening me? I can't let him know of my suspicions...

"Two weeks, you said? Why two weeks? Why my father?" I ask as innocently as possible. I don't want this crazy old man to think I'm questioning him, interrogating him, when in fact, that's exactly what I'm attempting to do.

"I don't have all of the answers," Merlin says gravely, shaking his head, "but you must trust me on this—if you do not fulfill your quest, your father will die."

Now that *definitely* sounds like a threat. I can't hold it in any more. I'm not going to stand here and let someone I don't even know threaten me and my family.

"What's really going on? Is someone going to try to hurt the president, to *kill* him? How do you know all of this? Maybe *you're* the enemy!" I jump up screaming, pointing Excalibur at Merlin's throat. This is all too shocking. Yeah, maybe I lost my cool a little bit, but I can't believe anything this crazy old man says. *He* must be the one plotting against my father, against the United States of America!

"My father, whom you seem to know so much about, warned me about crazy old men like you! You're trying to brainwash us! Well, I'm not buyin' it, man! We're going to leave now," I grab Gwen's hand and start backing out of Merlin's, I mean, crazy old guy's, cult den. "Don't try anything funny and don't try to escape. I'm remembering every detail about your face and the police will stop you before you can do any real damage!"

Gwen and I make our way out of the den while "Merlin" stays quietly and calmly seated on the dirt floor. He has a disappointed look on his face, but doesn't say a word until Gwen and I are out of his lair and running toward the Fun House.

From behind us I hear him yell in an unshakable voice, "Miles Arthur, you are wasting valuable time! Remember the King's Scabbard! You have only two weeks!"

Only when Gwen and I are entering the passageway back into the Fun House do I look back, Excalibur still tight in my hand in case the old man somehow catches up to us. But he doesn't. In fact, as Gwen takes the lead and is now pulling me deeper into the safety of the Fun House, I see, or think I see, the old man taking a mason jar in his hand and smashing it in front of his feet, disappearing into the giant cloud of blue smoke that results.

Gwen and I make our way out of the Fun House even faster than we had gone through when we were running away from Kay. The insane old terrorist who calls himself Merlin seems a much more dangerous threat than Kay could ever be. Gwen and I only stop running once we are out of sight of the Fun House and on the opposite side of the fair near all of the farm animals.

It takes a few minutes for us to catch our breaths.

"I'm surprised no one said anything about me

running around with a giant sword," I say, still holding Excalibur. The old rags that Merlin used to cover it were left somewhere around his den. I guess I could really use a scabbard.

Gwen is still breathing heavily. "This...is...a...state fair..." she says between breaths. "A kid...running with...a sword...is not nearly...the weirdest thing... here."

I laugh. "True," I say, knowing the oddities that abound in this carnival atmosphere.

"Do you really think that old man is a terrorist? Or that he's a cult leader or trying to hurt the president or something?" Gwen asks, now back to her normal breathing.

We walk around the livestock displays. The place is empty; nearly all of the animals are asleep. Perfect place to figure things out, except for the awful smell...

"He must be," I say, but truthfully, I really don't know.

"I'm not so sure. How do you explain him knowing so much about us? Our names, your family—he knows more about you than I do," Gwen says, squeezing my hand.

"He probably stalked us. The more he knows about us the more worried we should be. He probably knows where we live and has been following us for a while."

"Okay..." Gwen still sounds doubtful. "And what about the imagery vortex thingy?"

"You said it yourself—we're at a fair. There's plenty of weird things to see. It was probably just special effects of some kind." Some pretty good ones.

"And 'The Sword in the Stone' game that only

worked for you? And that medieval sword in your hand?" Gwen asks.

I hold up Excalibur. It certainly does appear to be from the Middle Ages, and it's the best sword I've ever seen. It would put everything else in my dad's armory to shame.

"I don't know," I say, truly puzzled. "Just some kind of recruiting trick, some brainwashing technique to get us in his cult. You know, give us gifts, tell us we're kings and queens, then next thing you know we're tied up in his little den for ten years, or worse, he makes us his slave workers and sends us out to do his dastardly deeds. OOooooOOOOOh!" I make a ghostly noise, trying to cheer up Gwen so she's not too scared, although I myself think any of these scenarios are quite possible.

"Stop it!" Gwen says, playfully shoving me. "This is serious! What are we going to do?"

"Tell my dad what happened, I guess. He's in the Secret Service, you know, and he used to be a Navy Seal."

"Yeah, I know," Gwen says. Apparently she does know something about me. Probably heard Kay boasting about everything in school. He's always bragging about his amazing life to everyone, trying to impress them. And it usually works.

"Dad will know what to do," I say confidently.

Chapter Fourteen

I'm wrong. Unfortunately, Dad doesn't seem to believe a word I say about the whole ordeal, and Kay won't back up my story at all! His pride must be so hurt by not being able to beat "The Sword in the Stone" and watching me do it, twice, that he won't even admit he saw the old man or the game at the fair.

"Okay, then how do you explain this?" I say, handing Excalibur to my dad.

"He bought that thing. I saw a vendor selling them. I almost didn't let him bring it home. He could've damaged the car."

Kay has an answer for everything, or should I say, a *lie* for everything.

"Did not! I won it! Excalibur was the prize for beating 'The Sword in the Stone!'"

"Excalibur? Is that what you call this sword?" Dad asks, studying the blade.

"Yes, Dad, because it is Excalibur. *The* Excalibur!" I explain.

"Mhmm. Well it *is* a fine piece of metalwork. One of the finest I've ever seen, in fact. And it certainly appears old enough to be from the early Middle Ages. But tell me something, Miles. If you didn't believe a word this crazy old man who believes himself to be Merlin said, which I certainly hope you didn't, then why do you believe this sword is really Excalibur?" Dad asks.

"Well, I...uh..." Good question. I hadn't really thought of that.

Kay smiles. "Exactly," he agrees with my father and acts like he came to the same logical conclusion himself.

Yeah, right.

"Well, whether you bought the sword or won it, it's yours," Dad says, handing it back to me.

"But Dad!" Kay shouts.

"I wasn't addressing you, Kay," Dad says sternly, not even turning his gaze from me and the conversation we are having.

Kay backs down like a submissive dog.

"And I will contact the appropriate authorities regarding the old man. State fair employees really shouldn't be filling young children's heads with nonsense." Dad leaves the room, probably to make phone calls to his various friends and contacts in the various police, protective, and investigative services clustered around D.C.

Kay and I are still seated at our enormous dining room table.

"You're lucky that crazy old coot didn't kill you and your little girlfriend," Kay says, standing up to go to his room and to bed. It's already one in the morning and the night's been full of too much excitement, but I still need to know something.

"You couldn't just tell Dad the truth?" I ask.

Kay just shrugs as if it doesn't matter one way or another and walks out of the room. What a jerk.

* * * *

The next day, Saturday, Dad wakes me up really early by storming into my bedroom.

I sit up in bed, squinting in the bright morning light. Dad has an angry look on his face. "What's up, Dad?"

"There was nothing at the fair, Miles. Nothing behind the Fun House. No 'Sword in the Stone' game and no den filled with jars and candles. In fact, there wasn't even a passageway in the Fun House leading to the back of the fairgrounds and no skinny old man with an incredibly long, silver beard works for the fair. Nobody's even seen a person matching that description in the area, so next time you decide to make up some fantasy, keep it to yourself, tell your friends, or write it down, but don't waste *my* time."

Dad doesn't wait for an explanation—as if I had any. He just leaves, slamming my bedroom door on the way out.

I pick up my cell phone to call Gwen. I made sure I got her number before we left the fair last night, just in case any important developments occurred. Well, I consider this important.

"Hello?" Gwen answers softly. She sounds like she was sleeping. She sounds lovely.

"Gwen? Hey, sorry if I woke you. It's Miles."

"Yes, Miles, I know."

"Oh, right. Duh. Anyway, my dad just woke me up

and told me there's no trace of the old man. Not a thing. And nobody's even seen him before. *And* he says there's no passageway leading to the back of the Fun House!"

There are a few moments of silence.

"Gwen?" I ask.

"That's really weird, Miles. What do you want to do?"

"I don't know. What do *you* want to do?"

"Ugh. I hate this game. Just make a decision," Gwen says.

"Okay..." wow, very straightforward. I kind of like it. "I say we go to the fair and see if we can find anything ourselves."

"Okay," Gwen agrees.

"Oh..." I realize something.

"What?"

"I forgot. I have no money," I admit, completely ashamed.

"It's fine. I'll cover it," Gwen says.

"No, I couldn't ask you—"

"You didn't ask. I offered. And I'm telling you. Pick me up in an hour."

"Oh, uh..."

"Let me guess," Gwen says, "You don't drive?"

"I'm only fifteen!" I say.

"Okay, I'll pick *you* up in an hour."

"All right. Do you know where I live?" I ask.

"Of course. Everyone knows the Ector Estate." Gwen says "Ector Estate" with a hoity-toity accent. Of course she knows. Kay brags about everything.

"Okay, see you soon," I say. "Wait! How can you drive? Aren't you fifteen?"

"Fourteen, actually. And you can't get in trouble if you don't get caught." Gwen hangs up.

Wow. My kind of woman.

Gwen picks me up twenty minutes late. Not too bad for a teenage girl, from what I've been told. Not that I would know.

She's driving an old Buick she says her parents hardly ever use any more. They won't even notice it's missing.

We get to the fair and head straight to the Fun House—after Gwen pays both our entry fees, of course, still to my utter embarrassment—but there's nothing to see. Dad was right; there's no passage leading outside to the back. In fact, where there were three passageways to choose from last night, now there are only two!

"Really weird," Gwen says.

"Yeah," I concur.

We even ask around to see if anyone remembers a skinny old man. We leave out the fact that he had a shiny, silver beard because—who knows?—that could have been fake, too, but no one has seen him. Most of the carnies are overweight or relatively young.

Gwen and I even walk around the perimeter of the fairgrounds to check out the back of the Fun House. Again, nothing. No sledgehammer game or den, no evidence of our experience with crazy old "Merlin" whatsoever.

"Well, what now, Sherlock?" Gwen asks as we drive back to my place.

"Nothing, I guess."

I sigh. What can we do?

Chapter Fifteen

I don't see or talk to Gwen for the rest of the weekend. I'm too busy training. And it's extra brutal. Dad must be getting out his frustration with my "lying" by making me work extra hard. Usually weekends aren't too bad, but Dad must be trying to teach me a lesson. Weekends tend to be stamina work with outdoor activities—camping and survival techniques and whatnot. But all Saturday—after I got back from the fair with Gwen—and Sunday this weekend I spend getting my butt whooped by Kay in everything from boxing to balance beam jousting. He must still be angry, too, because his hits are extra hard and my body is extra bruised by the time Monday rolls around.

But roll around it does and back to school I go, more sore and broken than usual.

I pretty much zone out the whole morning, my usual routine, the only thing that keeps me sane.

I'm just moseying along through the hallway, staring at my feet, trying to go unnoticed, when someone blocks my way.

I look up. It's a kid I don't recognize just standing right in front of me.

"Oh, sorry," I say, stepping to the side to walk around him. But he steps back into my path.

"Excuse me," I say, trying to move the other way. Again, he blocks my path.

"Can I help you?" I ask, not quite knowing what to do. I don't pick fights, I'm not aggressive, but I'm about to lose it.

The kid just smiles. I've never seen him before but he looks really odd. He's wearing ratty old tennis shoes that seem to have no brand whatsoever, frayed jeans, and a plain white T-shirt. His hair is some unidentifiable color, not really blonde, not really gray, but almost a white color, like a pearl or opal in strand form. But the strangest thing of all is his eyes—pools of gray that twinkle with iridescent sparkles and convey a sense of ancient wisdom. I've seen these eyes before...

"Are you..." I can't bring myself to say it, but I already know.

Merlin smiles and his eyes glow even brighter.

"I do love a good transformation trick!" his voice is as deep and aged as ever.

Gwen notices me talking to this strange person in the hall and walks over.

"Hey, Miles. Who's your friend?" she asks innocently.

Merlin winks at me. I remain in stunned silence.

"Do you not recognize me, my dear?" Merlin asks.

"Merlin!" Gwen recognizes him immediately.

Merlin does the odd little jig that he seems to not be able to repress whenever he's really excited.

"Stop it!" Gwen instructs sternly. Surprisingly, Merlin obeys. "Boys, come with me."

Gwen moves quickly down the hall. We have no choice but to follow. She leads us down into the art wing of the school. Art, yearbook, the school newspaper, photography, even drama class are all housed in this wing. I've never been down here before for a couple of reasons: one, Jesuit High is a huge school—it's home to over four thousand students—and there's no time to wander around campus between classes to anywhere else other than the classroom where you're assigned, and two, I'm not allowed to take any art electives. Dad makes sure of that. Only extra gym classes, like weightlifting, for me.

Gwen opens the door to the photography classroom, then leads us to the darkroom and practically shoves us in. There's a dim red light on, one just bright enough for us to see each other.

The bell rings. Guess I'm not going to Biology today.

"Okay, we're good. It's Mr. Bennett's off period, so nobody will be coming in here. He always leaves to smoke in his car," Gwen says.

I laugh. Teachers being bad is just funny to me for some reason.

"So, I'm assuming you're here to convince us to find the scabbard?" Gwen asks Merlin. Apparently, she's taking charge of the situation. Fine by me. I have no idea what to do.

"Why, yes, of course. If you don't fulfill your destiny, who knows what would happen? Certainly not I," Merlin says.

Gwen looks at me. "Listen, Miles. I've been doing some research. All of the old legends about King Arthur seem to agree—the scabbard is really important. And you can't deny this is the real Merlin anymore. I mean, look at him! A crazy old terrorist wouldn't be able to turn himself into a kid!"

I look at Merlin. "True... how did you do that, anyway? And how did you get into the school?"

"To answer the latter question, do you really believe schools are hard to get into or out of? Please. Any child can do it and for an old man with plenty of experience *disguised* as a child, well, it's a piece of cake. As to the former, transformation tricks have always been Merlin's specialty!" Merlin says proudly.

"Yeah, but really, like *how* did you do it? How did you learn to do magic like that?" I ask.

"Why, by studying, my boy, of course. There are special books, libraries, even schools for all types of subjects, even magic, *secret* though they may be," Merlin says.

"Like Hogwarts?" Gwen exclaims, clapping her hands together in excitement.

Merlin rubs his brow. "No, not like Hogwarts. We don't fly around on brooms or take trains from imaginary platforms. The world we live in has enough magic, more than any of us can ever discover or master in a hundred lifetimes. No, the magic books, schools, and kingdoms all exist in our very own plane of existence. No need to move into other realms." Under his breath, though I can't see his lips move in the darkness, I think I hear him mutter, "Not yet, anyway."

"Oh..." I think I understand. "So it's like the school for X-men. It's not in a separate world, it's just secret?"

Merlin slaps his head in disbelief. "Kids these days.

Fine, if it helps you to think of it that way, fine. But I warn you, your lives and adventures are *not* fantasy. You are not comic book cartoons. There's real danger and real consequences, whether you succeed or fail."

"Okay, then what do we need to do?" Gwen asks in all seriousness.

"The quest for the King's Scabbard involves three separate yet integrated tasks. You must show leadership on the battlefield, courage when alone, and cunning when needed. Only then will the Lady of the Lake give you the scabbard, or should I say, only then will you be able to *take* the scabbard from her!" Merlin stops. There is silence.

"Um...that's not very specific..." Gwen says.

I was thinking the same thing.

"Oh, well, uh... Yes, it is difficult to predict the exact circumstances, of course. But remember, you must always be chivalrous and gallant!" Merlin says awkwardly.

"What the heck does that mean? Do you even know what you're talking about?" Gwen yells angrily.

"Well, um...in all honesty, there is a bit of the myth that remains unsolved. I have not quite yet put together the whole puzzle..." Merlin admits.

"Ya think?" Gwen says rather rudely.

"Pardon me, madam, but would you like to try your hand at translating the Scroll of the Lake?" Merlin answers defensively, pulling out a crinkled, cracking, rolled-up piece of paper. I have no idea where it came from. He never seems to have or use any pockets. It's like he just pulls things out of thin air.

Gwen takes the scroll. "Sure. Why not?"

Merlin scoffs. "Pardon my asking, my lady, but

where did you receive your education in translating ancient tongues?"

Gwen laughs. "Nowhere. I don't need it. It's called a translation app." She pulls out her phone.

Huh. Wish I had thought of that.

Gwen takes a picture of the scroll with her phone. The app she has can apparently translate text from a photo. I look over her shoulder. It identifies the script as a coded form of blended Aramaic, Sanskrit, Latin, and Greek.

"No wonder it was so hard for you to understand," Gwen tells Merlin, who is grumbling to himself in a corner.

"Wha, what?" he says, jumping up and coming over to look at Gwen's own version of magic. "I had no idea these devices could be so useful. I tend to stay away from electronics and other modern technologies."

"No kidding," Gwen says. "Well, the scroll says this:

'*Three tasks of chivalry shall be done,*
for he who claims to be the one.
Three tokens of proof must be provided,
for sword and scabbard to be united.
For leadership in battle the token shall be
armor of the defeated, no less than three.
Courage alone can only be shown
with bodily scars to be forever known.
Cunning of the mind is most important of all,
outwit the Lady or be doomed to fall.'"

"I guess that's a little more helpful," I say.

"Kind of. Looks like you had the gist of it, Merlin,"

Gwen says in a conciliatory tone.

"I am more helpful than a silly electronic toy!" Merlin grunts, still upset that he was outdone by a phone. "Can your 'app,' as you call it, tell you *where* the Lady of the Lake may be found? Is there an app for that?"

Gwen and I can't stifle our laughter at his involuntary joke.

"Sorry, Merlin. You just quoted an old commercial," I explain.

He looks confused and not amused.

"Never mind. No, of course, you are more important, more valuable, than any app, phone, or tablet. You're my advisor. I trust you," I say, trying to smooth things over.

Merlin's eyes twinkle. "Ay, sir. And when you are King I shall remain at your side. Royal Advisor is what I am best at! Now, as to the tasks, you must complete each as quickly as possible. Then you shall go to the Lady of the Lake. She can be found in an ancient forest glen in what is known to you as Yellowstone National Park."

"Yellowstone! But that's in North Dakota or something!" Gwen says.

"Wyoming, actually. And part in Montana and Idaho," I say. Wow. I'm surprised I know that. I guess the fact somehow stuck in my brain from geography class or something for some reason.

"And?" Merlin asks.

"That's *really* far away! We're in Virginia, ya know. How are we supposed to get all the way to Wyoming?" Gwen asks.

"I am sure I don't know, but I am absolutely positive that you must make it there in twelve days," Merlin says matter-of-factly. "Oh, but you must also make it back and get the scabbard to Sir Ector, remember. Still, it should be no great obstacle given modern convenience and advances in transportation."

"Twelve days? I thought you said we had two weeks," I say.

"Quite right. Two weeks from when I told you about the quest. But since then you have wasted two days. You must make haste! Now you only have twelve days and Sir Ector must be holding the scabbard on the twelfth day from today, that is to say, on Saturday, October the fourteenth, at 2:17 p.m., precisely."

"I thought the magic time would be midnight. You know, like Cinderella?" I say in another attempt to be funny.

No one laughs. Merlin looks at me with utter seriousness.

"2:17 p.m., precisely."

"Okay, okay. Jeez."

"Remember the tokens and beware your half-sister!" Merlin yells, and at the same time he jumps high into the air, landing feet first in a tray of liquid used to develop photographs. Only he doesn't land—he disappears straight into the liquid, without making a splash!

Gwen and I lean over the tray and peer in. A photographic print lying flat at the bottom of the tub slowly develops. It is Merlin, in his common form of skinny old man with a long beard wearing a robe and holding a staff, only he is making a funny face, purposefully crossing his eyes and giving himself bunny ears with his free hand.

"Wow. He is a little bit crazy," I say.

"No kidding," Gwen agrees.

Chapter Sixteen

"So, what now?" Gwen asks.

We're driving to my place, having decided to skip school for the day. Gwen's driving, of course. This old Buick sure comes in handy. And Merlin was right—getting out of school is a cinch!

"Well, I guess we better start on the quest. We only have twelve days!"

"Yeah. But how are we supposed to go to battle? The scroll said you have to fight in a battle. People don't just start battles for fun. At least, not anymore," Gwen says.

"I don't know. What I'm worried about is getting to Wyoming." I sigh. It seems impossible.

"Why? That's easy. We'll just take my car," Gwen says, surprisingly nonchalant about the whole thing.

"Um, what about school? What do we tell our parents?"

"Jeez, Miles. Quit being such a worry wart. I'll take care of it."

I don't know what to say. Take care of it? Take care

of it how? This is my first time skipping school, let alone ditching for two weeks. I don't think my dad'll go for it, whatever excuse Gwen is going to come up with. I know he won't.

We pull up my half-mile long cobblestone driveway. Gwen parks right in front of my house. I don't have the heart to tell her to park in the garage. I'd be too embarrassed if she sees all of our fancy cars and I force her to park her Buick next to them.

"Does it ever get old, Miles?" she asks, looking up at my three-story mansion.

"What?" I ask.

"Living here. You already live like a king. No wonder you're going to become a real one, or already are one, I should say."

"Ha! Yeah right. The place is nice, but it's more like a prison than a palace."

"I'd rather live in a prison like this than in my tiny place. It's a shack and my parents still never notice whether I'm there or not... Well, let's get goin'!" Gwen hops out of the car happily.

She stares in awe at everything in the house as I lead her up to my room. No one's home, of course, except my mom and our maid Felicia, but even if they noticed Gwen and I here they wouldn't say anything. They wouldn't even think anything were wrong or out of the ordinary. They're both kind of out of touch with reality in their own ways...

"Cool! A bearded dragon!" Gwen says, running over to the terrarium in my room.

"What's its name?" she asks.

"Archimedes."

"Ha! It would be!" she laughs.

"So, I don't think we should leave tonight. I think we should plan out the trip in detail, get our supplies together, and start early in the morning," Gwen says, flopping down leisurely on my bed.

"Um...we're leaving for Wyoming tomorrow?" I ask in surprise.

"Of course! Quests always involve adventuring across the land, traversing long distances, looking for dragons and damsels in distress! You really should read up on yourself, Miles. A little research into the legends of King Arthur might do you some good," Gwen says.

"Oh, like you're the expert!" I say, sitting next to her, not daring to lay down.

"Hey, at least I skimmed the Spark Notes!" she says.

"Great... Hopefully you're better at getting me out of this house. What *is* your plan for that, anyway?"

"Oh, that. Yeah, I can take care of that right now if you want," she says, taking out her phone. "Should I talk to your mom or dad?"

"Well, my mom will believe anything, but my dad won't even believe what *she* tells him, so you better talk directly to my dad. But I have to warn you, he's smart and can't be tricked. I don't think this will work—whatever your plan is."

"Puh-lease. What's the number?"

"Okay, but don't say I didn't warn you."

I tell her his cell phone number and she dials from her phone, but it looks like she's dialing through some app, not just from her regular home screen.

"Hello, Mr. Ector?" she gives me a thumbs up at my dad having answered. I just shake my head, expecting the worst, but Gwen is speaking in a professional, adult voice. She's not overdoing it, it doesn't sound fake, so maybe there's a chance...

"Yes, this is Mrs. Parker from Jesuit High School. It seems Miles has forgotten to inform you about his upcoming trip to Boston for the Heritage Club. The permission slip was due today, so I'm calling to make sure you can sign it if I fax it to you. Mhmm... yes... well, we'll be leaving tomorrow by bus, you see, so it's very important to get this immediately."

Wow, she's good!

"Mhmm... yes, he's right here." Gwen hands me the phone. I feel the blood rush to my face.

What? I can't do this! She was supposed to take care of it! I'm an awful liar!

Gwen has a look of urgency on her face and elbows me in the ribs. I take the phone.

"Hello?" I say nervously. I can hardly keep a steady voice. This is never going to work!

"Miles, I'm way too busy to be dealing with this sort of thing. I can't believe you're not even responsible enough to get a permission slip signed on time. No, I take that back. I *can* believe it, I just don't want to. Have Mrs. Parker fax the form to my office. You're lucky I'm even in the office today. Put Mrs. Parker back on."

"Okay." I hand the phone back to Gwen. I'm still shaking.

"Hello?" Gwen says, back on with my dad. "Yes...yes sir, right away. I'll be sure to. You have a nice day as well. Buh bye." Gwen hangs up, smiling proudly. "Easy. Told you."

"Um, yeah, but what about the permission slip? And

what if he tries calling the school to verify or something? I'm still not sure this will work."

"Ugh, Miles. Such a nervous Nellie. It's quite unbecoming! I'll use the slip I always use with my parents. I'll just change the dates. It's very professional. He'll buy it. And the app on my phone makes the incoming call number on your dad's phone show up as the school's number, so he won't suspect a thing."

Hmm... Maybe this will work.

"Okay, wait. What about the fax? Won't the fax number show up wrong?"

"No. I'll have Jenny fax it from the school so it will be legit. She works as an office assistant. It's good to have friends in high places." Gwen texts Jenny with the necessary info. In only a few minutes, she gets a text back.

"Done. Have fun, girl! ;)"

"See? Easy!" Gwen says confidently.

I think I'm in love.

Chapter Seventeen

As Gwen and I are preparing for our journey—packing food rations of mostly canned goods, dried fruit, nuts, and a few treats just for fun, and camping supplies such as sleeping bags, a tent, waterproof matches, lanterns, and flashlights, all of which we have in my underground bunker storage area since Dad's always prepared for everything, including nuclear war—a text comes through on my phone, which I'm only allowed to use in emergencies. It's from Dad, and it says: *"Trip for POTUS. Vacation detail, pre- and post-sweep. Home in 2 weeks."*

This happens a lot. The President decides to go on a trip and Dad has to go secure the site, guard the president while he's there, then make sure everyone leaves safely. He's a busy guy and this time his hectic work schedule works for me.

"Perfect!" I show Gwen the text. "Now we can stay here for the night. One more night in civilization before the quest!"

To be honest, I'm actually looking forward to living on the road for a bit. I've never been on an adventure before.

"What about your mom and brother?" Gwen asks, shoving another can of tuna in her already stuffed bag.

"Please. They hardly ever notice I'm home. And they never come in my room," I say.

"Same with my parents."

We finish packing and load the supplies in the Buick. The car is so big that even with our twelve days' worth of supplies—along with some extras, just in case—stuffed in the trunk and back seat, there's still enough space to comfortably fit another person.

"You should probably move the car behind the gym. Just so no one sees it and suspects anything," I say.

"Okay."

Gwen pulls the car around back and then we head back to my room.

"I still have to train with Kay just so he doesn't suspect anything. He'll be home any minute."

"Okay. I can entertain myself. I'll just play with Archimedes, read, think about our future children…"

I look at her in surprise. "Really?"

"No, you weirdo!" Gwen shoves me playfully, a twinkle of her own in her beautiful golden eyes. "Get out of here! Try not to get beat up too badly!"

"Will do," I say smiling.

I walk down the hall and downstairs, not able to get the image of Gwen in my room out of my head.

Chapter Eighteen

But Kay's not in the gym. In fact, he's nowhere to be found; not at the shooting range, the garage, the armory, and there's no answer when I knock on his bedroom door. I think about calling him, but he would probably just ignore my call.

As I'm getting two sodas from the fridge for myself and Gwen, wondering where Kay could possibly be, he suddenly comes bounding through the front door with scores of his football buddies behind him. They are all carrying various party supplies, from disposable cups to giant bags of snacks. A couple of guys are even dragging in a keg.

"Put it by the pool," Kay directs the guys with the metal barrel full of booze. Only then does he notice me.

"Hey, Miles! Ready to party?" he actually looks and sounds happy. Not really happy to see me, but just excited. Giddy, even.

"Um...what are you doing?" I ask.

"Didn't you get Dad's text? He's gone for two weeks! It's time to throw down!"

"What about Mom?"

"She's out of town, too! Some alumni fundraiser or something in New York. We have the house to ourselves, bro! It's perfect!"

Kay goes out by the pool to make sure everything is in order. I follow.

"But it's a Monday!" I say, still in disbelief that Kay would actually throw a party. In this house. With Dad being Dad!

"So?" Kay says, putting the keg in a tub of ice.

Good point. Kids at our school will party any night of the week.

"Well, have fun," I say. Kay already knows I won't try to stop him and I won't tell Mom or Dad about the party. Why should I? He's my brother and he's a kid. He's allowed to have some fun.

I start to walk back into the house to go to my room. Kay yells, "You can have fun too, ya know! Maybe even get lucky! I hear Leanie's coming!"

I pretend not to hear and hurry back to my room. Leanie? That's not good. Not only because Gwen is here and I don't want Leanie ruining that, but because the last thing Merlin said to me before disappearing into a photo was to beware my half-sister. But why? He didn't really explain. He didn't explain at all, actually. Maybe he knew Leanie would try to ruin things between Gwen and I, just because she's a girl and girls are like that. Jealous and low self-esteem and everything. So should I even tell Gwen she's coming? I don't know...but I better decide soon...

"What's all the noise out there?" Gwen asks as I enter my room.

"Kay's having a party. Apparently *both* my parents are out of town."

"Cool! I love parties!" Gwen says, running over to the door.

"Um, should we really go out there? I mean, we do have to get started early in the morning. Ya know, go cross country, save my dad, that whole thing?" I also don't want Gwen to see what a nerd I am and how I don't have any friends, although she probably already knows. Still, I don't do very well at parties. I'm too shy, I guess.

"We don't have to go crazy or anything. We can still have fun," Gwen looks at me with uncompromising puppy dog eyes.

"Ugh...fine." I give in. I can't say no to this girl.

"Yay! Thank you, Miles! I promise it will be fun!"

I doubt it, but what can I do?

* * * *

People really start showing up around nine o'clock. All types of kids, not just football players and cheerleaders—drama kids are here, band kids, kids who don't do anything at all. Kay knows a lot of people, but some of these kids definitely aren't in his clique. I guess word of mouth really is a powerful thing.

Kay doesn't even try to keep everyone outside on the pool deck—there's way too many raucous people to control. My parents' room is the only thing off limits in the house. The garage and armory are obviously locked up, too, but the hundred or so people who have shown up are pretty much scattered all over the estate.

"Hey, Miles!"

I turn to see who called my name out on the pool deck. It's Baldwin Bretagne, a really weird kid whom I unfortunately have a few classes with. Even though I don't have any friends, I'd rather be a loner than have Baldwin hanging around me, always sniffling and itching the back of his neck and smelling kind of funky. But I'm not rude, so I can't ignore him.

"Hey, Baldwin," I say, trying my best to sound not completely annoyed with his presence.

"Sweet place," he says, pointing around with his awkward lanky arm. His gangly arms and legs, always hanging out from clothes too small for him, have even more freckles than his face, the tree-bark color of which matches his scraggly hair almost perfectly.

"Yeah, it's pretty nice."

"So, how's it going?"

"Um…good…"

"Yeah? Cool."

Obviously neither of us are good with conversation.

"I didn't know you liked parties."

Baldwin looks at me awkwardly. "I don't."

"Then what are you doing here?" I ask.

"I invited him," Gwen steps next to us out of nowhere.

"Oh. Okay. Why?" I ask, not trying to sound rude, though I kind of did.

"Because he's the smartest kid I know, at least in regards to legends and myths. I thought he might be able to help us plan our trip."

"Actually, Mr. Malory knows more than me, but I guess you couldn't really invite him to a high school party!" Baldwin laughs piggishly, thinking about our English teacher hanging out with us, but he suddenly gets a serious look on his face and leans close to me, so close that I can smell his funk.

"I hear you found something. Something *special*," he whispers.

"Huh?" I ask, not knowing what he's talking about.

"Baldwin, just come out and say it. He wants to see Excalibur," Gwen says.

"Oh, sure. It's in the armory. Let's go."

We leave the boisterous party behind and walk to the armory. It's a good thing we have so much land and space between us and our neighbors, otherwise the cops would probably have been called by now.

I scan my hand to let myself into the armory. These kinds of fancy locks are on all the important rooms in our house, so I've kind of gotten used to it, but Baldwin is astounded by the novelty of the thing.

"Wow! Sweet security system!"

"Thanks."

Baldwin's excitement with the hand-scanning lock is quickly replaced with even greater astonishment as he walks into the armory.

"Oh—my—gosh!" Baldwin pulls out an inhaler, fumbles around with it, then finally gets it to his mouth for a quick puff as his eyes nearly bulge out of his skull at the sight of the Ector family's collection of weapons.

"This way," I direct, not wanting to give an hour-long tour to the kid.

We get to the medieval section of the room where my dad had hung Excalibur on the wall.

"Oh my… Can I…touch it?" Baldwin asks nervously.

"Sure," I say. But just as I remove the sword from its display and go to hand it to Baldwin, a loud, deep horn sounds from outside, vibrating the very ground I'm standing on, stopping me in my tracks.

Chapter Nineteen

"What the heck was that?" Gwen asks, looking as frightened as I feel.

"I don't know. I guess we better go find out." I walk out of the armory, Excalibur in hand, Gwen and Baldwin following closely behind.

I open the front door. I don't see anything out of the ordinary. I thought maybe the odd sound was the police with some sort of megaphone trying to get our attention, but there isn't a cop car in sight, just the assorted cars of all the kids who came to the party cluttering the driveway and lawn. But then I do notice something out of the ordinary—silence. No party music from the pool deck. All is quiet.

"Come on!" I say, grabbing Gwen's hand and running to the back of the house, Baldwin trailing nervously.

Everyone is gathered on the pool deck and standing still, utterly motionless, looking out to the backyard and woods. Coming out of the forest, across five hundred yards of perfectly manicured lawn, I see what appears to be hundreds of torches being carried by men in medieval armor. Even from this distance I can hear the clank of metal on metal, the rattle of chain mail, the marching of a hundred heavy boots. The dark army stops a few paces out from the tree line. From the middle of the line of men, eleven knights on horses ride out. Their armor shimmers in the moonlit field. I can hardly believe they're real.

"We demand the one who claims to be king! We demand Arthur!" one of the knights on horseback yells at us, a bunch of kids at a house party.

Everyone looks around at each other, nervously confused. There are some whispers. Nobody knows what to do.

Suddenly a big kid stumbles forward to the front of the crowd. It's Spencer, and he appears to be a bit wobbly on his feet.

"And who're you?" he yells back at the dark army, seemingly fearless as he slurs his speech.

"We are the rightful heirs to the kingdom and we demand Arthur!"

"Well then, sir—*hiccup!*—you need to ask—*hiccup!*—nicely!" Spencer practically trips over his own feet as he hollers at the unknown foes.

"Boy! You have no idea who you are dealing with! Now send out Arthur!" The dark knight is apparently not amused.

"I—*hiccup!*—would like to know what you're going to do—*hiccup!*—if I don't!" Spencer stumbles around aimlessly, waiting for an answer. There is silence across the field.

Spencer turns around to address the still stunned

crowd of high schoolers. "See! *Hiccup!* They're a bunch of sissy actors!"

Not a second after Spencer finishes speaking, an arrow comes flying out of the sky, unheard and unseen in the black of the night, and strikes him directly in his left calf with such force that it rips through his shin—the tip can be seen sticking out of the front of his leg. His leg has been shish-kabobed.

"AHHHH! WHAT THE—!"

Spencer's scream is drowned out by the yelling, screaming, and running of the hundred or so kids who witnessed the event. They are all running for their cars at the front of the house, pulling out their phones to call the police, their parents, or both. But no one's screens light up. Everyone's phones seem to be dead and won't turn on, not even mine.

I run with everyone else, not sure what else to do. I don't think I can leave my own house, especially with those crazy people in the backyard trying to find me and willing to shoot high schoolers to get me, but I'm panicking and just follow the crowd.

When I reach my driveway, I see that nobody's cars are starting, no matter how many times they try to crank their engines. Some kids try to make a run for it, but as soon as they reach the end of the driveway, I see them fall to the ground twitching, as if they've been hit with a stun gun. When the others on foot see their friends who were ahead of them now convulsing on the ground, having run into some kind of force field, they stop. Some run back to the house for safety, others try to help their downed friends, dragging and carrying them back to the house as well.

I go back inside, still trying to figure out what to do. Everyone's gathered in the foyer at the front of the house. Kay has brought in a hobbling Spencer and lays him on the floor. A girl starts trying to tend to his wound as best as her high school first-aid training will allow. The kids who were shocked by the force field are all laid gently on the floor as well. They seem to not be twitching as much, but are still unconscious. Everyone looks pale and afraid, not knowing where to go or really what's going on. Some girls are crying and shaking. Even some of the boys have tears in their eyes.

I have to do something. This is my house, my castle, and those people outside are after me, after all.

"Everyone... Everyone!" I yell, finding my voice. "Listen up! I'm not really sure what those people out there want, I'm not sure really what's going on, but I'm going out there to find out! Just wait here. I'll be back."

I start walking to the back of the house, my heart beating loudly and quickly. I feel a hand on my arm. I turn around and see Gwen. She looks scared, but in a steady voice says, "I'm going with you."

I want to say no, but for some reason, I don't. I know she wouldn't listen, anyway. Her eyes are determined.

"Miles! You dropped this!" Baldwin offers me Excalibur, kneeling on the ground and holding out the sword to me hilt-first, like a proper squire.

"Thanks," I say, grabbing the sword. "Sure you don't want to come?" I ask jokingly.

"Really? You'd...you'd let me?" Baldwin asks, actually smiling at the suggestion.

"Um, yeah. Sure. The more the merrier," I say, not able to hide a smile myself. He's such a weird character.

"Wow! I've never been part of an a priori parley before!" Baldwin exclaims. He immediately tears off a big piece of fabric from the white-upholstered love seat that was already dirtied and ripped from the party. He then pulls down a curtain rod, quickly affixes the cloth to one end by wrapping it around the pole a few times, and then begins to carry it like a flag. I would normally object, but I have more important things to worry about right now than a dismantled curtain and piece of busted furniture.

"Uh...a what?" I ask, not knowing what Baldwin is talking about.

"Pre-battle negotiations!" Baldwin says, running ahead of Gwen and I in his odd excitement.

Chapter Twenty

The three of us walk down the back stairs of the pool deck—Baldwin nearly speed walking, hunched over in his awkward gait as he carries his makeshift flag with pride, then me with Excalibur held tightly, both palms sweating, and finally Gwen, looking around in all directions nervously, probably trying to spot any stray arrows, or worse yet, perfectly aimed ones.

The dark army hasn't moved from the tree line and the eleven shadowy knights are still out front, about a hundred yards in front of the rest of them. Apparently they knew we were all trapped and had decided not to move or attack any further.

Baldwin is the first to speak when we reach the eleven on horseback.

"Noble sirs, it is my pleasure to introduce the young and rightful king, the heir to the throne of men, the monarch by birth, blood, and divine right, the one and only one who removed the sword from the stone, his Grace, King Arthur!"

Silence.

Gwen and I look at each other. Suddenly, the eleven knights burst out laughing. We can't see their faces, but their wolfish cackling pierces the gloom of the night heinously.

"Boy, your fancy speech is better served in court than the battlefield! Haha!" the knight who seems to be the leader says.

My cheeks start burning with anger and embarrassment. Good thing no one can tell in the darkness.

But Baldwin is apparently unflustered. He shoots back, not missing a beat, "You do yourself a disservice, *sir*, not giving due respect to your king!"

The lead knight makes his horse take a few steps forward. He looks huge, towering over us. They all do.

"No *boy* is my king! I am King Lot and we eleven have earned our lordship through birth, blood, and battle. Any who wish to reign must do the same!"

The colossal man looks at me. I can barely make out his dark, bearded, scarred face through his helmet, though he certainly looks menacing enough. Or is it just my imagination creating this countenance inside the pitch-black helm? I can't really tell...

"Now, hand over Excalibur, renounce your kingship, and we shall let you live."

"Never!" Baldwin shouts, having stepped in front of me, preventing me from even considering the dark knight's offer.

"Then you shall all die!" King Lot, as he called himself, rears his horse and goes galloping back to the tree line with the rest of the eleven leaders.

Baldwin, Gwen, and I begin running back to the house, Baldwin dropping the white flag of truce along the way, not knowing how long we have before the battle begins.

"Nice going, Baldwin! Now we're all going to die!" Gwen pants as we continue sprinting as fast as we can.

"Nonsense! We have the king on our side! We have Excalibur! Miles can't die while wielding Excalibur!" Baldwin says confidently.

"I'm no king and I *can* die! It's the *scabbard* that can protect me, not Excalibur!" I explain as we reach the pool deck.

"Well, duh. So what? You'll still be protected," Baldwin says, holding the back door to the house open for Gwen and I.

"No, because we don't have the scabbard! That's the whole point of the quest we are supposed to be taking! The quest is *for* the King's Scabbard, but now we're all going to be killed before we even get started!" Gwen yells.

Baldwin looks at her apprehensively, slowly coming to understand the truth of our dangerous, potentially deadly, predicament.

"Yeah...that could be a problem."

Chapter Twenty-One

Baldwin, Gwen, and I start moving slowly toward the main entrance room where everyone is still gathered, trying to come up with a plan as we go, but before we even reach the foyer, we hear tremendously loud crashes and rumbles. The whole house shutters. It's like an earthquake.

"Trebuchets," Baldwin says, a bit too calmly in my opinion, given our situation. "It's cool, we should be all right for a while." He smacks the wall he's closest to and looks up at the ceiling. "Reinforced cinderblock. Good construction. Perfect for resisting an artillery attack. Yup, a modern day castle. This baby will hold for days."

"And what about when they decide to storm the castle? You know, charge with the cavalry and send in the infantry, swords drawn, spears ready to spike us through our unarmored bodies, decapitation, disembowelment, the works?" Gwen yells.

Gruesome stuff.

"Hmm...yeah...that could be a problem," Baldwin replies.

"Listen. We need to come up with a defense strategy, and fast! You both saw the armory. We have plenty of weapons. We even have plenty of people. We just have to come up with a plan," I say, pausing before the portico archway.

"Plenty of people? It's a bunch of high schoolers who just wanted to party! They don't know a thing about fighting or weaponry!" Gwen screams.

"Then we'll just have to teach them," I say, walking into the foyer. Everyone looks at me as soon as I walk in, a hundred pairs of frightened, teenage eyes.

Well, here goes nothin'.

"All right everyone, listen up!" The trebuchet projectiles continue to pound and rattle the house. "Those people out there mean war. They're serious. They want to kill us all." A few girls begin crying. Even some of the guys are holding back tears again. "Now obviously we can't escape. We can't even call for help. They have some kind of force field surrounding us and obstructing our devices. So our only option is to fight!"

Everyone suddenly starts yelling, crying, complaining, whining, and arguing. Not the reaction I expected.

"Listen! Listen!" I try to command the room, but everyone has gotten into such a frenzy that it's no use. Some kids are still frantically trying to get their phones to work, others run out the front door to try their cars or their luck on foot again. I'm sure they'll come back disappointed, but there's no stopping them. Everyone has gone wild with fear.

"Well that didn't work," I say, returning to Baldwin and Gwen, the only sane people left.

"Yeah. Now what?" Gwen asks.

"You must rally them, your Highness. Rally them to your cause!" Baldwin says bravely.

"I just tried! You saw what happened!" I exclaim.

"Not with words, your Grace. With action! A king leads with action!"

I think about this for a few moments. Baldwin's right. Actions speak louder than words.

"You know, you're pretty good at this, Baldwin. Whatever *this* is," I say smiling. Somehow, Baldwin inspires confidence, at least in me, and that's really what I need most right now. Confidence and courage.

"Thank you, my Liege," Baldwin says, kneeling before me.

"Get up, you fool!" I say, pulling him to his feet. "To the armory!"

Chapter Twenty-Two

The three of us rush to the armory as the trebuchets continue raining down chunks of rock onto my house. It sounds like giant balls of hail weighing hundreds of pounds apiece are falling onto my roof, but so far Baldwin seems to be right. The roof and walls are holding strong.

"What do we need?" Gwen asks, ready for her orders like a true soldier.

"Guns. Definitely guns," Baldwin says, rubbing his hands together greedily like a kid in a candy store. Not the reaction I expected from this nerdy guy, but hey, what do I know? I didn't expect my house to be assaulted by medieval knights, either.

"Can't. My dad keeps the ammunition in a separate safe that only he has access to. As a precaution. None of the guns are loaded and I can't get the bullets," I explain.

"Darn!" Baldwin exclaims, seemingly more disappointed in not being able to fire one than out of concern for our battle strategy.

"Then what are we going to do?" Gwen asks.

"We're just gunna have to fight them mano-a-mano with *their* style of weaponry. Grab everything you can!"

I start pulling swords and spears off of the wall. Baldwin and Gwen follow suit.

"Let's go!" I yell once everyone's arms are full. I lead the charge, not to the yard for battle, but to the garage for further preparation.

"What are we doing in here? The cars aren't working, remember?" Gwen pants, dropping her weapons to the floor.

"Yeah, I know. But I know something that *will* work."

I pull a tarp that was covering my surprise, revealing a soapbox-derby-style vehicle big enough to fit two people.

"Um... what's *that*?" Gwen asks, utterly perplexed.

"It's a go-kart I built when I was a kid. One of the few things my dad actually let me do that I wanted to do. I convinced him it would be good for me to learn how to build things and..." I point to the inside of the vehicle, "it would be good exercise."

Baldwin and Gwen lean into the vehicle to see that I'm pointing at the foot pedals which power the vehicle like a bicycle.

"No electronic parts included—or required," I say.

"Interesting," Baldwin says.

"Now, here's the plan. There's a nice size hill on the west side of the backyard. It's a perfect starting point to gain speed and the backyard actually contains a series of smaller hills that slope downwards toward the valley on the east, so we should be able to keep a pretty fast pace. We should be able to get to the western hill secretly enough as long as we stay on the far side of the yard. It will be best for two of us to go. One to steer, one to fight. The third person should make a distraction on the east side of the battlefield. That way the enemy will think they're surrounded and panic. Maybe even some of Kay's friends will join in and fight once they see what we're doing," I say optimistically, though I'm really not.

"This is really happening, isn't it?" Gwen asks.

"Yes. But we'll be fine," I say as confidently as I can. I touch Gwen's shoulder and even manage a smile in an attempt to comfort her.

"Okay, so what's the distraction?" Gwen asks.

"Oh, yeah. Duh. We'll use these." I run to the opposite side of the garage and uncover an extremely large chest. Gwen and Baldwin sprint over to look. I pop open the top.

"Wow! That's a lot of fireworks!" Baldwin shouts.

"Yeah. Kay would normally kill me if I touched his stash, but under these circumstances, I think he'll understand. So, Gwen, you're in charge of the distraction. Baldwin and I will take Bertha and the western flank." I get odd looks. "Oh, that's what I named the car. Bertha."

"No way. I'm going with you. And *Bertha*," Gwen says.

"Gwen, I..." I begin to argue but am cut off.

"I'm going with you, Miles. I'm sure I'm more experienced at driving than either of you," Gwen says firmly.

"It's true. I've never driven before. But I do love explosives!" Baldwin says, still staring at the chest of fireworks, apparently mesmerized by the abundant collection.

"You? Explosives?" Gwen asks, as shocked as I am at the revelation.

"Oh, yes. I'm a bit of a pyrotechnic pyromaniac, you might say," Baldwin chuckles.

"Okay, then. I guess that's that. Let's go get set up!" I say. I run to the back of the garage and grab a toolbox and several rolls of duct tape.

"We have to outfit Bertha to be battle ready. Let's get some spears sticking out in all directions and reinforce the wheels. Cover the outside with as much armor as possible," I direct. Gwen follows her orders amazingly well as we get started immediately.

"I'm going to rework some of these fireworks. Combine some powder, rewire some fuses. Should make a much better show!" Baldwin says, sitting down to get to work.

"All right. You've got fifteen minutes," I say.

"Aye, aye, Captain!" Baldwin says jokingly.

"That's King to you, boy!" I laugh, slapping Baldwin on the back happily and getting back to work with Gwen. It feels good to be in high spirits before a fight—for once.

* * * *

In fifteen minutes, everything's ready. We've had to make a few trips back to the armory for more supplies, but now we're fully prepared for battle.

"All right. Let's do this. Good luck, Baldwin," I say, shaking Baldwin's hand. I'd slap his back again, but he's wearing a backpack full of his recently re-arranged explosives. He made so many that he's even wearing a backpack on his front side. He said it's much easier than running with a crate full of them, and safer, too. I'm glad to just be taking his word on this one.

"God speed, my King," Baldwin says, and he's off. In three minutes, he's going to start the show, so Gwen and I must get going.

As I jump in the driver's seat to conserve Gwen's legs for the battle, Kay comes into the garage.

"Miles! I've been looking all over for you!"

"No time right now, Kay. I've got to go."

"What the heck are you doing? You can't go out there! They'll kill you! Didn't you see what they did to Spencer?"

"That's exactly why I've got to go. They'll do much worse than that if they breech these walls!"

Kay stands in front of Bertha, blocking my way. He looks frightened, more frightened than I've ever seen him before. In fact, I've never seen him frightened before. Not ever.

"Kay! If you want to help, go gather up as many people as you can and put weapons in their hands. When you see explosions to the east, attack. Now go!"

Kay's expression goes from frightened to determined in an instant. He steps aside to let Gwen and I pass.

"I'll do what I can. Good luck, brother."

I pedal out of the garage, immediately feeling the extra weight of the now fully-armored and battle-prepped Bertha. Kay goes running inside to gather the troops.

"Well, here goes nothin'," I say as we make our way slowly along the west side of the estate.

"Yeah, here goes nothin'," Gwen says quietly.

C.E. Zyburo

Chapter Twenty-Three

Amid giant pieces of rock hurdling through the starry sky, amid the sounds of clanking armor in the distance, and the seemingly heavy breathing of the dark knights waiting to attack, waiting to charge, waiting to kill, amid torchlight and moonlight, Gwen and I, in a stealthily moving Bertha, make it to the top of the western hill, unnoticed. Only one minute until the fight of our lives begins. Literally.

We switch seats so that Gwen can steer. She won't have to do much pedaling with the speed we're going to gain from the steep downward slope of the hill. In fact, I told her that once we get going, she should lift up her legs entirely out of the way of the pedals to let us gain full speed and not risk getting her feet ripped off because they are probably going to be spinning as fast as helicopter rotor blades.

We put on some medieval armor for extra protection and I put a lance in my lap with plenty of other long weapons lying between us. Excalibur sits solidly at my side.

"You look good," Gwen says shyly.

"Thanks," I reply.

We have nothing more to say. The seconds tick by silently as we wait for Baldwin's signal. It seems to take forever. We see shadow after dark shadow fly overhead, the outlines of the rocks being flung at my house from the enemy trebuchets.

Suddenly, to the east, comes a loud whistling sound. A bright trail, the kind that usually streaks vertically from under a launching firework, moves horizontally across the tree line. A huge ball of bright fire explodes directly in the middle of the line of dark knights.

"That's the signal!" I yell over the commotion of more explosions and shouting of the surprised enemy knights.

Gwen gives one big push with her legs and we're off. She lifts her feet out of the way of the furiously spinning pedals. I ready my lance, lowering it out of the side of the flying vehicle, aiming straight ahead with deadly ferocity.

"Smooth ride!" Gwen yells sarcastically over the loud rumbling and clanking of the wood and metal reinforced box that is our war chariot.

"I know, right?" I yell back.

We must be travelling forty miles an hour by the time we make it halfway down the hill in this thing that wasn't built for such speed.

"Hey, how is Baldwin gunna know where we are? How to aim away from us?" Gwen asks.

Huh. Didn't think about that.

Our gazes meet. She sees I don't have an answer. We both turn back, looking straight ahead, ready as we'll ever be for the chaos ahead.

And chaos it is. We reach the first enemy knight standing twenty paces in front of the tree line Gwen is expertly skirting. She sees him and veers in his direction. He doesn't even see us coming. I aim my lance and brace for impact. I hit him just below the shoulder on his right-hand side. The impact is severe and sends a shockwave through my body, but Bertha hardly budges and doesn't slow down a bit, having so much inertia from the steep hill and all the extra weight of the armor and weapons.

I look at my lance. It's broken. I toss the end and as I'm grabbing another a huge fireball explodes directly in front of us. Gwen veers sharply to the left, narrowly avoiding the explosion, so narrowly, in fact, that I can feel the heat and ash on my face.

I miss the next knight as I'm still trying to recover from the crazy swerving and blinding explosions, but I get another one in the leg as Bertha continues rocketing down the line.

I grab a spear for my next weapon. Moving to the proper position, I see that in a few seconds we'll be plowing through the eleven lead knights on horses.

"Uh... Gwen! I don't think this is such a good idea!" I yell, fearing our little soapbox car is no match for eleven war horses mounted by battle-hardened knights.

"Okay! Hold on!" Gwen yells back, but we continue our screaming beeline toward the leaders.

"Gwen! Gwen!"

At the last possible moment, Gwen pulls a hard right to narrowly avoid crashing into the eleven knights. Bertha, despite her extra armor weight, rolls onto her two left wheels like a drifting stunt car.

"AHHHH!" Gwen and I scream, but we end up back on all four wheels and are still travelling quickly, although I know we'll be running out of steam now that we're facing home and running diagonally against the slope of the field.

I look behind us. The eleven mounted knights are charging, slowly gaining ground as Bertha's careening speed runs out.

"Keep heading for the house!" I tell Gwen.

"We're not going to make it!" she yells. We're still several hundred yards away and losing speed fast.

"Start pedaling as fast as you can and keep her steady!" I direct, and without wasting another instant, stand up and begin hurling every weapon I have at the knights getting ever closer. I hit one directly with a spear and he falls from his horse.

"Yes!" I congratulate myself on my surprisingly accurate throw, quickly grabbing another spear to throw. I miss with this one, but succeed in tripping up a horse, sending his knight flying through the air which, as luck would have it, trips up yet another horse, bringing his knight to the ground as well.

"All right! Two for one!" I celebrate, but my victory is short-lived. The knights realize my game and adjust, spreading out to make themselves harder targets and not prone to the domino effect.

"Miles! We're not gunna make it!" Gwen reminds me, having checked behind her and seeing the knights only fifty yards back, the relative safety of my house still over a hundred yards away.

"Just keep pedaling! We have to try!" But I'm worried, too. Still, better to make it as close to the defense of the house as we can before I have to stand and fight, eight dark knights against one me.

As I aim another spear, probably my last before I have to abandon Bertha for ground combat, a firework comes flying out of the east and hits a knight right in the helm, exploding on contact into a brilliant fireball of red. A barrage of fireworks follows, striking here and there, occasionally hitting a knight or horse. This must be Baldwin's grand finale! There are so many explosions that I can hardly look. It's like staring into the sun. But I can tell that those few knights who are left on horseback are having a difficult, if not impossible, time controlling their horses. Some have lost all control and are struggling even as their horses retreat back into the woods out of sheer animal fear and instinct.

"All right Baldwin! We're gunna make it!" I tell Gwen, jumping back into my seat.

Gwen is still pedaling furiously and is almost entirely out of breath.

"Yeah...so...how do we...get him...back?" she asks, panting between words.

Oh, shoot. I didn't think about that.

Chapter Twenty-Four

Bertha rolls up to the pool deck, Gwen using every last ounce of energy to pedal her there. We get out and run into the house. I can't believe Gwen hasn't collapsed from exhaustion!

The hail of rock from the trebuchets has stopped entirely now that the dark army is leaderless. I can see that two of however many there are out there are on fire thanks to Baldwin's expert aim and mastery of explosive engineering, but I don't take time to stare. We have to get out there and make sure he's safe.

Gwen and I get to the foyer, but it's entirely empty. Then we hear the clanking of metal, the now familiar sound of medieval armor and weapons.

"Oh, no," Gwen whispers, shuddering and clutching my arm. "We're too late."

But from the side door into the foyer come not enemy knights but a hodgepodge of oddly-equipped high schoolers. Some are wearing helmets and carrying spears, their gym shorts showing from below ill-fitting chain mail; some girls have only breast plates and swords for protection, their fully made-up faces and ribboned hair still showing their youth and innocence; others wield nothing but baseball bats, but they all have one thing in common—inexperience.

Kay is at the front of the group and spots me instantly.

"Here's your army! It may not be the best, but they're all ready to fight. The unwilling ones are safe in the armory."

I look at Kay in disbelief. I can't believe he got this many kids ready to fight. Boys, girls, nerds, jocks—almost everyone is ready for battle. The vast majority of the kids at the party are willing to fight, to fight for me, despite their inexperience, their utter lack of knowledge of what they're getting themselves into. Yet I have no choice but to let them fight. To lead them into battle. It's fight or die.

"All right, everyone!" I take command, a confident, brave voice coming forth that I didn't even know I had. "There's a brave young man out there who's risked his life to save ours, to prolong ours. He's out there alone, he's out there still fighting, and we're going to save him! Those enemies out there, the enemies that have attacked us without warning and without reason, they will be taught justice! *We* will teach them justice! Let us fight! Let us fight NOW!"

"YEAH!" The crowd ecstatically erupts in unison.

I turn to Kay and whisper amidst the shouts, "No time for battle tactics. I'll lead the troops. You and Gwen go find Baldwin. Look to the east in the direction of the fireworks."

Kay looks disappointed that he won't be leading the charge, but he follows my orders. "See you soon," he says, grabbing Gwen's arm and running off to complete his mission.

"CHARGE!" I yell to the troops, not wanting to delay, not wanting to waste their newly realized fervor and zeal.

We run out of the house, across the pool deck, and onto the battlefield. Nearly a hundred rushing bodies, pumping with adrenaline, ready to fight to the death. I normally would have been overtaken by now by much faster kids, but I too am being propelled by adrenaline and seemingly some other energy I can't describe. I continue running full speed in front of everyone, the others fanning out in either direction like a great human wave with myself at the middle of the pointed crest.

We run and run, across the entire lawn, passing only dropped weapons and empty armor. We reach the tree line, ready for battle, ready to meet any enemy that may be waiting, but there are only the dark outlines of the trees and the crackling of the burning trebuchets casting dim, flickering light on more abandoned armor and weapons. There's no enemy to be found.

Baldwin, Gwen, and Kay join me at the front of our now silent and still group, but I'm too shocked and confused to embrace Baldwin or properly thank him for his service. I'm still looking around, waiting for a surprise attack or at least the showing of our enemies.

"Where is everyone? I know I'm good, but I'm not *that* good," Baldwin says, breaking the silence.

"I don't know," I reply nervously, still cautiously eyeing the forest ahead of me.

"I do!" booms a voice from the shadows within the trees.

I lift Excalibur in front of me, ready for a fight.

"Who's that? Show yourself!" I command the bodiless apparition.

Out of the darkness steps a tall, thin figure, his blue robe blowing in the gentle breeze, his long beard somehow hanging stiff against it.

I lower my sword.

"Merlin!"

Chapter Twenty-Five

"AHHH!" Moose, Kay's idiot friend, charges at Merlin with an ax, not realizing he's a friend.

"No!" I yell, running to block Moose's blow with my sword. But I'm a step behind, too far behind.

I think this is the tragic end of Merlin, but I'm wrong. He lifts his staff rather calmly to block Moose's blow. As soon as the wooden shafts touch, Moose's ax turns into a Styrofoam noodle, the kind little kids use to swim in the pool. Moose stumbles and falls to the ground, having lost his balance with the loss of weight when his heavy ax turned into a nearly weightless toy.

Merlin steps to the side, letting Moose fall, but the noodle still whips him right on top of his silvery head.

"Ouch! You fool! That hurt!"

He rubs the spot, seemingly not caring that he just nearly died.

"Merlin! What the heck are you doing here? What's going on?" I ask, still out of breath from the whole affair.

"I'm right where I'm supposed to be. As are you. I

couldn't have missed the Battle of Bedgrayne even if I had tried!"

Baldwin smacks his forehead. "Holy smokes! The Battle of Bedgrayne! I just lived through, I just *fought* in, the Battle of Bedgrayne! Utterly astonishing..." he says with wide-eyed amazement.

"Um, I'm still lost," Gwen says.

"Yeah, me too," I say.

"And I'm sure all of your friends are as well." Merlin motions behind us.

I turn around. Oh yeah. I almost forgot about the nearly one hundred kids at my back.

"Perhaps we should go inside," Merlin suggests.

"Good idea. I'm pooped," Baldwin agrees.

As we, all hundred or so of us, begin the slow march back across the field of battle, Merlin begins to explain what happened, and what's still happening. Except for the sound of footsteps, all is quiet. Everyone even tries to quiet his or her breathing so as not to miss a single detail. This is the most important thing any of us has ever been a part of.

"Over a thousand years ago, the Battle of Bedgrayne..." Merlin begins slowly, secretively, a sound of darkness in his deep voice, "was the first battle that King Arthur ever fought. It was a battle against eleven kings of the north, rebel lords who denied Arthur's right to the throne..."

As Merlin speaks, mists begin to creep out of the ground on each side of our marching assembly of kids. The mists form two eerie walls of smoke we're able to pass through, walking in between the walls with Merlin at our front like Moses leading the chosen people through the parted Red Sea. Unlike the walls of the Red Sea, however, images begin to form on our misty walls that become clearer and clearer as Merlin continues to speak.

"Back in medieval times, the rebel lords attacked Arthur on his anointing day, laying siege to his castle."

This image forms on the misty wall to our left. We see an ancient castle being assaulted by enemy troops, trebuchets firing boulder after boulder, an enemy army being led by eleven dark knights on horseback.

The medieval battle on the left continues to rage silently, but the image on the right wall comes into clearer focus as Merlin continues, "And this night, over a thousand years later, the rebel lords attacked Arthur again, for the very same jealous reason that drove them to war so long ago..." the moving images on the right wall of mist show what occurred only moments ago—the dark army appearing out of the forest in my backyard and attacking my house.

"But!" Merlin yells excitedly, "The brave noble, the one true king, would not stand for such treason! He rode out among his enemies, Excalibur in hand, prepared to fight to the death!"

On the left wall, a proud young king rides out onto the battlefield on a noble steed, sword glistening in the sun, ferociously striking down his enemies as he rides. On the right, the misty wall shows Gwen and I in Bertha riding out to meet the dark knights. As Gwen steers around the endless explosions of fireworks, I drive my enemies to the ground with lance and spear. I look to the group of high schoolers behind me, embarrassed by my actions, no, embarrassed by the *showing* of my actions in such a display. But everyone behind me is gawking at the moving images on the walls of mist, absorbing everything they're seeing, listening to everything Merlin is saying, in stunned silence.

"Arthur's bravery, his gallantry, his *leadership* on the battlefield, saved him, his men, his castle. Arthur proved himself that day, each of these days, proved that what was his right by birth was also his right by deed!"

The image on the left showed the proud king of the past, myself in a past life, standing triumphant on a hill overlooking the battlefield.

I look to the right to see what that image will be, but I suddenly realize I'm no longer walking in between walls of mist, but standing on the tallest, westernmost hilltop of my yard, the hill where Gwen and I started our charge with Bertha, overlooking our own battlefield now filled with our fellow high school students, all looking up at me. Merlin is at my side on the summit, beaming, yelling to the audience below, "My friends, you all have been chosen to serve the rightful king of the land, the king who will lead you to not glory, not gold, but peace! Peace, the long sought and dearly acquired! Peace, the treasure of treasures! Will you join him? Will you follow him?"

Merlin grabs my hand, the hand still holding Excalibur, and lifts it into the air.

"All hail King Arthur!" he yells, looking proudly over the field, ready for the responding chorus of cheers.

But there's nothing. There's silence. I think I even hear a cricket chirping, just like in the movies.

In the darkness I can just make out a few faces of the kids in the front of the crowd, and they all show confusion, some are upset, some just look plain tired.

"I want to go home!" some unseen person yells from the crowd.

There are nods and mumbles of agreement all around. Everyone starts to drop their weapons, take off their random pieces of armor, and walk toward the house. I stay standing on the hill, dazed, staring off blankly at the disbanding crowd. A few moments later I hear cars revving up. Apparently everything's back to normal. Or back to working order, at least.

I see Baldwin, Gwen, and Kay walking up the hill toward Merlin and I. We begin to trudge down to meet them.

"Well, that didn't go as I'd planned," Merlin admits softly, his forehead all squinched up in a perturbed manner.

"Yeah, neither did my first speech," I say.

The five of us walk into the house quietly—exhausted, embarrassed, and not knowing quite what to say. We get to the living room and all flop down on either couches or recliners. The whole house is empty now save for us. High schoolers sure do know how to abandon a party quickly.

Kay breaks the silence. "Well, that was fun. Now does someone mind explaining what's going on? A little more detail, perhaps, this time?" He stares untrustingly at Merlin.

"Ugh!" Merlin groans, his head in his hands. "Things used to be so much easier. People appreciated showmanship, especially kids! Now with all of these movies and video games, nobody gives a hoot about magic!"

"Yeah, yeah. This generation is lazy and worthless

and I bet you walked to school in the snow, uphill both ways! So sorry for you. But what about us? This house, our whole estate, is a mess, and there were people trying to kill us! Now tell us what's going on!" Kay yells, starting to get really angry now.

"What do you want to know?" Merlin submits tiredly.

"Well, for starters, who were those people out there?" Kay asks.

"The armies of the eleven rebel kings, of course. Of course they weren't *real* armies. Real knights don't fight in the dark. They can't see what they're doing."

"Not real knights? Then what were they?" Gwen asks.

"Oh, conjured images, much like mine, only with more substance I suppose. Dark magic can create such things," Merlin sighs.

"Yeah, more substance. I'd say so. My arm is pretty sore for having only struck images," I say, rotating my striking arm that hit several "not real" knights.

"Well it's not like they're holograms," Merlin snarls. "There *are* bodies in there, just not fully thinking humans, per se. They're not people, mind you. Just conjured bodies. That's why they disappeared."

"Zombies!" Baldwin yells excitedly.

Merlin smacks himself in the forehead. "No, not zombies! They're not the walking dead! They're conjured bodies!"

"Oh, sorry," Baldwin apologizes.

"Indeed..." Merlin grumbles.

"Well, what about the eleven leaders? I talked to them. They seemed pretty real to me," I say.

"Probably just stronger magic."

"Okay...then who did it? Who sent the 'conjured' army? Who's in charge?" Kay asks, frustrated with the answers he's getting.

"It could be a number of people, but my guess is it's his half-sister," Merlin points his thumb in my direction.

"No way!" I say. "Leanie's not that mean. She may be a little crazy, but she's not *that* crazy."

Merlin looks at me quizzically. "Leanie? Oh, Leanie! No, of course I don't mean Leanie! I'm talking about your *other* half-sister, Morgan LeFay."

Chapter Twenty-Six

"WHAT? *Another* half-sister? How many half-sisters do I have?" I ask in utter astonishment.

"Just those two, as far as I know." Merlin shrugs as if it's no big deal.

"Did you make out with this one, too?" Gwen asks with a scowl on her face.

"What? No! I don't even know who she is!" I say.

"Of course you don't. *I* don't even know who she is really. And she'll keep it that way as long as possible," Merlin says.

"Morgan LeFay? That's bad news!" Baldwin says.

"Why?" I ask.

"Because she's the most powerful enchantress in history! And she can shape-shift... She can be anyone or anything!" Baldwin exclaims.

"That's right. That's how she's eluded me all this time. I know she exists, that she's been reincarnated, just like all of us. Well, all of us except for Baldwin, anyway. But I don't even know what name she goes by now.

127

Certainly not Morgan LeFay. That wouldn't be good for one trying to exist in hiding!" Merlin says.

"Wait... Reincarnated? Who's reincarnated?" Kay asks.

Gwen quickly explains what Merlin had already told her and I, knowing that Merlin would take forever should we let him explain it. Kay's shocked by the revelation and sits back quietly, contemplating the magnitude of what he's just learned about himself and his family. Baldwin looks disappointed at first for not being a reincarnated soul, but then says, "Oh, well. Guess I'll just have to make a name for myself this go around," and waits attentively for whatever may come next.

"Okay, so my enemy can be anyone, anywhere, at any time. That's all well and good, but we still have to get the King's Scabbard and save Dad. We're going to start for Wyoming tomorrow. Can you help us, Merlin?" I ask.

"I will help in every way possible, my boy, but I'm afraid I cannot go with you," Merlin says, for some reason with a slight grin.

"Okay. Baldwin? How about you?"

"Of course, my Liege. Your wish is my command!"

"All right. Kay, you have to do everything you can to keep Mom from calling the cops. I don't want to have to elude a witch—"

"Enchantress," Baldwin corrects.

"Right... Enchantress...*and* the police while trying to save Dad."

Kay looks up at me, looking like he's still kind of lost in his own thoughts.

"All right, Miles. I'll do what I can," he finally agrees.

C.E. Zyburo

"Thanks, Kay. Well, Merlin, any advice before you go?" But as I turn back to him, he's already gone, apparently not willing to perform any more theatrics since his most recent failure. But where he was previously sitting is a note written in a messy hand which reads "You are well on your way, my King. Don't forget to collect your first token!"

I look at Gwen.

"'For leadership in battle the token shall be, armor of the defeated, no less than three,'" she says, repeating a part of the Scroll of the Lake.

"What? What's that?" Baldwin asks, surprised that Gwen seems to know something he doesn't.

Gwen hands him the scroll, which she has apparently been keeping safe and on her person at all times.

Baldwin looks at it, and is obviously confused.

"Oh, yeah," Gwen says, taking back the scroll and instead handing him her phone on which she has saved the scroll's translation.

Baldwin reads the translation quickly and smiles. "Wow! We've already completed a third of the quest! Sweet! And we're going to Wyoming?"

I nod.

"Awesome!"

"Do you need me to make an excuse for you? Ya know, like pretend to be the school and call your parents?" Gwen asks.

"Nah. I'll just tell them I'm going to check out colleges. Neither of them went to college. They have no idea how the process works," Baldwin says, taking out his phone to text his parents.

"Am I the only one without gullible parents?" I ask.

Baldwin and Gwen just shrug.

"Well, whatever works, works for me," I say.

"Done and done," Baldwin says, putting away his phone.

"All right. Let's go get some armor," I say.

Chapter Twenty-Seven

The next day, Baldwin, Gwen, and I hit the road, Gwen's old Buick now extra weighed down because of the three sets of armor we collected from the battlefield in my backyard. Oh, and I also decided to bring Archimedes in his travel terrarium. Couldn't leave him behind seeing as how I can't trust Kay to remember to feed him. And besides, he's my good luck charm.

We decide to take turns driving, six-hour shifts each, so that we make good time and don't get too tired. We're leaving six hours a day for non-travel to get gas, food, and sleep during the night, though we each plan on napping when it's not our turn to drive.

"GPS says it should take us just about twenty-eight hours of total driving time to get there, so at our pace we'll make it there in less than two days. If everything goes as planned, assuming we don't take too much time dealing with the Lady of the Lake, we should be back in Caerleon in five days tops. That leaves six days to spare, should anything go wrong. God forbid," Gwen says, looking up from her phone.

I'm taking the first shift driving. Even though Baldwin and I don't have licenses, we're taking our chances. People are out to kill us and my father, so driving without a license is the least of our worries.

My driving shift ends with nothing exciting to report. I go to the back seat to nap. When I wake up, the country outside is very different, not at all like Virginia any more.

"Where are we?" I ask.

"Ohio," Gwen says from the driver's seat.

"Wow. We're making good time," I say, stretching and yawning.

"Yeah, well, if we didn't have to be so cautious about following the dang speed limit, we'd be doing a lot better," Gwen grumbles.

"Better safe than sorry," I say.

"True," Gwen says.

Baldwin takes over driving somewhere in the middle of nowhere in Indiana. The sun's getting low on the horizon. We left at six in the morning with Gwen and I taking the first two driving shifts for a total of twelve hours. So far it's been smooth sailing.

But suddenly our luck runs out.

I hear the sound of police sirens first. Turning around, scared for my life, I see the flashing red and blue lights not far behind.

"Oh, no! What do we do?" I ask in a panic.

"Calm down and stop staring!" Gwen directs.

I turn my head forward, using every ounce of my willpower to keep from looking behind me.

"He'll probably pass us," Gwen says hopefully, keeping her eyes forward as well.

But he doesn't. The cruiser pulls up, fast, directly

behind us. Baldwin, paler than usual, pale as a ghost, pulls into the slow lane to try and let the officer pass. No such luck. He's on *our* tail. He's after *us*.

"What do I do, guys? What do I *do*?" Baldwin manages to squeak, his voice cracking nervously.

"Well, there's only one thing to do," Gwen says. "Miles, hand me something heavy."

I grab a breastplate of armor that's lying on top of the hoard next to me.

"That'll work," Gwen says, taking the armor. "I wish this POS had cruise control," she adds, leaning over toward Baldwin. "Lift up your feet," she says. Baldwin listens and Gwen craftily places the armor between his legs. "Miles, sit up as straight as you can. Make yourself as big as possible."

I do.

"All right, now comes the tricky part." Gwen gets into position. "Baldwin, when I say go, we need to switch seats as quickly as possible. I'll go low, you go high. Ready? Go!"

Gwen slides gracefully over into the driver's seat and Baldwin, not so gracefully, moves to the passenger's. Gwen picks up the breastplate from the floor, which was apparently holding down the gas pedal just right, and tosses it to me. I put it back on our pile of supplies, which, along with myself, was hopefully blocking the police officer's view of what just happened in the front seat. The whole escapade takes less than a minute, but unfortunately for us, that's a long time when you're being pulled over.

"Where'd you learn to do that?" I ask Gwen. She never fails to amaze me.

"I've pulled it once or twice before," she says modestly.

"Will it work?" Baldwin asks, still incredibly nervous.

"We're about to find out."

Chapter Twenty-Eight

Gwen pulls over onto the dusty shoulder, the police cruiser still right on our tail.

"Everybody be cool," Gwen says.

"What does that mean?" Baldwin asks.

"I don't know! It just seemed like the right thing to say!"

We're all staring into the rearview or side mirrors, waiting for the officer to emerge from his car. After what seems like an hour, he finally does. It's hard to see his face in the nearly non-existent light now that the sun's completely set, but it's obvious he's a giant of a man. His uniform is in perfect order, he's wearing sunglasses, and he puts on a wide-brimmed state trooper hat as he walks toward us. He doesn't look happy.

Gwen rolls down the window, cranking it the old-fashioned way. It creaks ominously, the window getting ever lower as the cop gets ever closer.

"How ya doin', officer?" Gwen asks sweetly, in a high-pitched voice that's not her own.

"You the owner of this vehicle?" the beast of a man asks in an extremely husky voice.

"No, sir. My parents—well, my mother, is."

"Mhmm…" the officer grunts.

"We're just on a trip, a research trip, really, to—"

"License 'n' registration," he interrupts.

"Yes, sir." Gwen pulls out the registration from the glove compartment, fumbles around in it for a few more seconds, and looks back to the officer with tears in her eyes. In a quavering voice she says, "Oh, no! I think I left my license at home!" She hands the registration to the cop, apparently hoping that will be enough.

He just grunts, then turns and goes back into his cruiser without another word.

"Is there somethin' wrong with that guy?" I ask to no one in particular.

"I don't know…" Gwen says quietly, staring at the rearview mirror, trying to make out what the officer's doing.

"Oh—!"

The screeching of the tires, the kicking up of the gravel and dirt, the rev of the powerful engine being pushed to its limit as Gwen floors it drowns out her scream.

"What? What?" Baldwin and I yell, turning this way and that, trying to see what Gwen's freaking out about. And then we do. Not only is there a police car behind us, but a huge, not very friendly-looking dragon!

"Go! Go! Go!" I yell to Gwen.

"What do you think I'm doing?" she yells back.

She's flying down the highway, I have no idea how fast, and I don't think I want to know. The monster behind us is coming on fast, having already crushed the police car under its massive weight as it clambered over it straight toward us. He, if it *is* a he, looks like he's trying to pick up enough speed to take flight.

He's running right at us, giant, dark auburn wings spread, body covered in glistening scales of the same hue. Suddenly he gathers just enough momentum and takes to the air, staying low, just above the ground to keep us barely out of reach.

"He's gaining on us!" Baldwin yells.

"I'm going as fast as I can!" Gwen screams.

"Well zigzag or something!"

Gwen swerves to the right just as a fireball comes flying past the car.

"Huh. I always thought dragons shot streams of fire, not fireballs..." Baldwin says.

"Baldwin! This is not the time to contemplate the historical accuracy of dragon tales! *Do* something!" Gwen says, pulling the car back into the fast lane. Luckily or unluckily, the highway's empty. I wonder if this is some kind of enchantment...

But Gwen's right. This is no time for contemplation. I have to figure out how to get rid of this dragon before he turns us all into toasted marshmallows!

"Right!" Baldwin yells.

Gwen swerves. Another fireball barely misses.

"Left!" Baldwin yells. Gwen turns and again we narrowly escape a fiery death.

Archimedes, in his travel terrarium, falls onto my lap from all of the crazy swerving. He's looking up at me, a crazed look in his eye that I've never seen before. He's clawing aggressively at the side of his terrarium.

"Miles! Do something!" Gwen yells, still flooring it and driving like crazy to save our lives.

But I'm too distracted by Archimedes to respond. Amid all the chaos, I just can't stop staring at him, and from somewhere in my head or due to some magic unknown to me, I hear a sweet yet commanding female voice say, "*Dominus opem ferat illi alae.*"

I take Archimedes from his terrarium and hold him lovingly in my hand. I crank down my window.

"Miles!" Gwen yells.

"*Dominus opem ferat illi alae,*" I say, and toss Archimedes out of the window.

Chapter Twenty-Nine

It immediately begins to rain and before Archimedes is out of my sight I see a luminescent raindrop shining with all of the colors of the rainbow hit Archimedes right in the middle of his back as he goes soaring out of the car. Exactly where the drop hit sprout two little wings, just big enough to help my little bearded dragon take flight and start soaring about.

The Buick continues shooting down the highway, so I expect to lose sight of Archimedes quickly, but somehow I don't. Then I realize why—he's getting bigger, fast.

"Miles!" Gwen yells at me again in an utter panic.

"Gwen, look! Look! It's Archimedes!" I yell, pointing at the now bus-sized bearded dragon flying next to us.

Gwen and Baldwin quickly turn and see what I'm so excited about.

"What the…" Gwen says in disbelief.

"By the diamonds of Solomon!" Baldwin exclaims.

Suddenly Archimedes branches off. He starts flying straight at the enemy dragon.

"Gwen! Stop the car! We can't leave Archimedes! We have to help him if we can!" I yell.

Gwen slams on the brakes. We come to a stop only after skidding a hundred feet, what with the rain, all of the weight of the car, and the lightning-fast speed at which we were travelling. I quickly hop out of the car, grabbing only Excalibur, and run toward the two already battling dragons.

The rain's coming down hard, but I can see the fighting beasts from their bright scales that seem not only to reflect light but even emanate some of their own.

The auburn dragon wastes no time in attacking my inexperienced Archimedes. He shoots a fireball straight at him. Archimedes has great instincts, though, and veers to the side, avoiding the fireball entirely. Unfortunately, although Archimedes is endowed with natural instincts, bearded dragons do not come with the ability to breathe fire, so he attacks the auburn dragon with his teeth and claws, tearing viciously at his enemy's flesh with ferocity I've never seen in him before.

The auburn dragon appears stunned to be engaged in such a battle. He must be used to raining fire and being attacked solely by frightened men on the ground. I doubt he's ever been met with aerial combat.

Now Archimedes has the advantage. He claws onto his enemy's back. Both beasts fall to the ground in a giant, snarling heap.

I come to a halt. If I get too close to the fight, I'll just be crushed into a jelly and then I won't be any help at all. Baldwin and Gwen stop at my side.

"Go Archimedes! Go!" Gwen yells, unable to contain herself.

C.E. Zyburo

"That's one heck of a pet!" Baldwin adds.

But I can't say anything. I'm too nervous for Archimedes.

My fears become reality as the auburn dragon suddenly overpowers Archimedes. He has him pinned, the full weight of his enormous body holding Archimedes down. The auburn dragon raises his head, ready to make his death blow.

I have to do something. Without thinking, I go charging in, Excalibur raised over my head.

"Miles, no!" Gwen yells, but it's too late. I'm running at full speed, ready to kill to save Archimedes.

The auburn dragon sees me and instead of delivering his deadly strike upon my precious pet, he sends a heaving fireball in my direction. It's all I can do to avoid being hit. Gwen and Baldwin narrowly escape as well.

From the ground where I dive to temporary safety, I look up and see my distraction has allowed Archimedes to escape. The dragons are now standing on two legs, fighting with claws and teeth, their long bodies curled up like snakes, then striking at any opening, drawing pools of blood as they tear off each other's scales and flesh.

I get on my feet, still feeling the searing heat from the fireball on my face. But I ignore it and charge again. I reach the auburn dragon and raise Excalibur to make a mighty slash at his tail, but either by reflex or design, he whips his tail at precisely the right instant, swiping my feet out from under me and sending me flying through the air, losing Excalibur as I fall.

I see Archimedes notice my danger and he's enraged. He now looks like he's the size of ten dragons and exhibits the power of ten as well. Archimedes leaps into the air and knocks the auburn dragon to the ground with his hind feet. He quickly jumps onto his fallen enemy and, wasting no time at all, bites onto his neck, gripping with such force that his enemy doesn't slowly strangle, but rather dies instantly with a thunderous cracking of his vertebrae.

Baldwin and Gwen rush over to me.

"Miles, are you all right?" Gwen asks, leaning over me, not daring to try and lift me up. She looks beautiful in the rain.

"Yeah, I think I'm okay," I say with a grunt, leaning on one elbow.

Archimedes comes rumbling over with such heavy steps that Baldwin and Gwen join me on the ground. He looks concerned and whimpers like a puppy at my side. I had no idea bearded dragons could make that sound, or act like that, or grow to such an enormous size for that matter!

"I'm okay, buddy. I'm fine," I say, standing up to ease Archimedes' worries.

He wags his tail like a dog, a giant dog that could kill me with a direct hit from his swooshing tail!

"Easy buddy, easy," I say, scratching his head as he leans over. "You did great."

And as I continue to rub him and soothe him, he shrinks and shrinks until he's his normal size. I place him on my shoulder where he clings as happy as can be.

"I guess his injuries aren't that bad," I say to Gwen and Baldwin.

"Yeah. More than can be said about *that* guy," Gwen says, pointing to the fallen auburn dragon.

We walk over to the body of the dead beast. Before

our very eyes the dragon begins to fade, turning into nothing but a pile of red-brown ash that washes away with the rain.

"Hmm. Guess that's why there are no dragons in the fossil record," Baldwin says.

Then a glint catches all of our eyes. A single, solitary dragon scale of brilliant color, the size of a knight's shield, is all that remains of the colossal beast.

Chapter Thirty

"Not a bad token," Gwen says as we all make our way back to the Buick.

I throw the heavy scale onto our pile of supplies and we all hop in the car.

"The dragon scale? That can't be the second token. The Scroll says '*Courage alone can only be shown with bodily scars to be forever known*,'" Baldwin explains, apparently having memorized the Scroll of the Lake after only one reading.

"So, what then? We fought a dragon just for fun?" Gwen asks, buckling up in the driver's seat. I guess she's taking over for the rest of Baldwin's shift. I join her up front as Baldwin is more than happy to relax in back.

"Well, to be fair, Archimedes did most of the fighting," I say, giving him a special treat of corned beef as I place him safely back in his terrarium.

"Okay, regardless," Gwen says. "We have two more tasks to do on this quest, and we *still* have to get to Wyoming and back, and we *still* have to get the scabbard to your dad on time. Isn't that enough without having to deal with dragons and other junk?"

Gwen starts driving and other cars magically appear back on the road, but before anyone has time to comment on the odd reoccurrence, a strange voice breaks in.

"My dear, a quest is not a thing planned. One never knows what one will stumble upon when out on quest."

Out of nowhere we all hear Merlin's voice, but he's not anywhere in the car. We can only see him in the rearview mirror.

"Merlin! Was that you who turned Archimedes into a giant dragon?" I ask.

"No, my King. I'm embarrassed to say that it was not. But lucky for you, you have other people who care about your wellbeing."

"Where are you?" I ask, not knowing if he's actually inside the mirror or just using it as a communication device.

"Exactly where I should be—forming alliances, checking facts, researching questions. I may have not *made* Archimedes grow, but I certainly helped to convince the person who did to do so."

"And who might that be?" Gwen asks.

"Nimue," Baldwin and Merlin say at the same time.

Merlin, from his place in the mirror, looks at Baldwin and scoffs.

"Indeed. Well, so you know about my apprentice. Yes, then you also know to what end I am doomed. But that is no matter now." Merlin gives Baldwin a look that seems to tell him to keep his mouth shut and Baldwin answers with a look of understanding and a simple nod.

Merlin turns quickly to address me.

"Yes, Nimue is my apprentice and a great enchantress herself. She has even developed some of her own magic, I dare say, and, luckily for you, sent aid while I was distracted elsewhere. I doubt not that a spell and conjuring potion were sent to you in your time of peril?"

"Yes! The words just came to me. And I saw a beautiful raindrop hit Archimedes and he sprouted wings!" I exclaim.

Merlin chuckles. "Haha! Yes, yes. Nimue enjoys a show nearly as much as I. But it's good that you now know how to wield the power of your King's Guard."

"My what?" I ask, not knowing the term.

"King's Guard, your King's Guard! One as valuable yet as despised as yourself cannot rely merely on *children* for protection!"

"Hey!" Baldwin and Gwen yell in unison, insulted that Merlin finds them unqualified to protect me.

"Hey is for horses! Haha! Yes, your '*hey*' would not protect your king from a dragon, no, nor any other great beast or creature of evil intent. But Archimedes! Oh, he will save you more than this once, my Lord, mark my words! Just say the words of the incantation, use a drop of the conjuring potion, and—poof!—Archimedes will not only grow wings but will also grow to enormous size to defend you, only to return to his normal, convenient size when the deed is done!"

"But I don't have the potion. It came with the rain!" I say, worriedly.

"Oh, yes, that. Of course. I knew I was forgetting something." Merlin fidgets with something out of view. "Ah! Here it is! Catch!"

From inside the mirror, Merlin tosses a small glass

vial that somehow passes through his side of the mirror and comes flying into the car. I catch it before it smashes into the back window.

"That, my boy—eh—my King, is the conjuring potion for your King's Guard, Archimedes. That's all of that type of potion known to man, all that's left on earth. I'd given a single drop to Nimue as a token of my love, and she has found it fitting to bestow it upon you in your time of great need—a noble gesture."

"OoOoOoOo, did someone say he's in *loooove?*" Gwen teases Merlin, having caught his accidental slip-up.

"Eh, what, what, what? Well, yes, perhaps, but it's no affair of yours! Now I must be off! Work to do, people to see, a king to save!"

"Wait! What about my dad? Do you have any more information about who's trying to hurt him? Or if it's the president who's the target? And what about my *real* family? You still haven't explained why I'm king or what I'm even king of!"

"Ugh... so many questions," Merlin groans. "You know, back in the Middle Ages, I would make one prophecy and then be silent, a tradition I fully intend to carry over now! So, what shall it be? Pick one question and be done!" Merlin commands sternly.

"Okay..." I have to think about this. Who knows where Merlin will appear next? Or when.

"I got it! How will I die?"

Gwen makes a weird squeaking sound as soon as she hears my question. Baldwin inhales deeply and says, "Miles, some things are better left unknown, or at least, unspoken of."

"What? Everyone dies. I just want to know how I will

die because if it's not on this quest, then I know we will succeed. I'll die before I fail at this quest," I reason, but it seems to do no good to calm anyone's nerves.

Merlin remains stern from inside the mirror. "Your mind is black and closed because you cannot see yourself failing without death, but many fail on grave tasks and still do not die. But you, my King, you are destined to make one with child whom you do not love, and that child will grow up to destroy your knights and your kingdom and you."

"What are you saying? Are you saying I will fail at this quest?" I ask, more worried than ever.

"I have made my prophecy. You will have a clean and honorable death, but your own son will destroy you."

With these disheartening words, the rearview mirror from which Merlin was speaking fogs over with a blue mist and shatters. He's gone.

"Great," Gwen says in a shaky voice, seeing her broken mirror. She rips it from the windshield, angrily cranks down her window and tosses it out. She looks as if she is holding back tears.

"What's the matter?" I ask. "Oh, come on. You can't believe everything Merlin says. He's not the *real* Merlin any more than I'm a real king. He can be wrong, you know. If I know the manner of my own death, maybe I can avoid it!"

"No. It's there as surely as if it had already happened," Baldwin says stoically from the back seat. He is gazing straight ahead with empty eyes.

"Guys, really? You can't be serious. I don't even have a son and I probably never will!" I can't believe Gwen and Baldwin are so upset right now. I can't believe that *they* believe in Merlin's prophecy. But they do. Their worried, depressed faces and thoughtful silence says it all.

"Psh, whatever. Well *I* don't believe it, anyway. You guys are fools," I say, angrily crossing my arms to give them a taste of their own medicine—that is, the silent treatment.

"Merlin was right. You have a black and troubled mind, my Lord," Baldwin says, still looking forward without expression.

I turn my gaze out the window. Gwen focuses on the long road ahead. We all drift off into our own unhappy thoughts.

Chapter Thirty-One

We pull over for the night after a few more uneasy hours of driving. We're all exhausted, not only from the trip so far, not only from fighting a fire-breathing—well, fireball shooting—dragon, but also from brooding over our own dismal thoughts for so long. We're all still upset, though I can't really say why. I guess the stress of the quest, of the great weight of the task so suddenly thrust upon our shoulders, is already weighing us down.

We start setting up our camp on a deserted back road in the country somewhere in Iowa. It would be too dangerous camping right next to the highway and we don't have money for hotels. Besides, camping isn't so bad. It's a cool night, the stars are out, and there are plenty of trees around for privacy to do…well, you know what.

I unroll the two sleeping bags Gwen and I packed—oh! That's right! I just now realize we only packed enough stuff for the two of us. Baldwin came on the quest on a moment's notice with no supplies or anything. He must really believe in me to come so unprepared, without knowing where he'll get food or shelter or clothes...

I walk over to him where he's setting up a ring of rocks to encircle our campfire. I hand him some loose-fitting clothes of mine that will still be too small for his long, gangly limbs, but I suppose no worse than the ill-fitting clothes he normally wears.

"Here, you can sleep in these. And you can have my sleeping bag and stay in the tent if you want," I say, deciding to end our pointless feud.

Baldwin looks up from where he's kneeling. He smiles.

"No way! You and Gwen stay in the tent. I'm fine in the Buick. It's plenty big. I'll take the clothes, though!"

Gwen comes walking over to us from the edge of the woods where she's been gathering firewood. She drops the pile into Baldwin's stone circle.

I step over to her and embrace her, giving her a long, tight hug. Slowly her arms move up and surround me in return.

"I'm sorry," I say. "Sorry I was so rude before. We have a long way to go and we shouldn't fight."

I pull away and look at her. Tears are streaming down her face.

"What? What's wrong?" I ask, wondering if she's hurt or still mad or what.

"Why'd you have to ask how you're going to die?" she cries, looking at me with such sorrow that my heart just drops. I feel awful, like the worst person in the world, for having caused this beautiful girl such pain.

"I'm sorry—I—I just thought it would help. I thought

it would answer two questions at once. I thought it would tell me whether or not I succeed on this quest."

"You're not the only one on the quest, you know. You're not the only one who cares whether you live or die!" She wipes away tears from each of her perfect cheeks.

I take her hand. "I know, Gwen. I'm sorry. But at least we don't have to worry about dying on this quest, right?"

She pulls away. "You mean *you* don't have to worry. Merlin didn't say anything about me or Baldwin, but he *did* say that you're going to have a son with someone you don't love!"

Gwen goes running off toward the forest. I start to follow, but Baldwin grabs my arm.

"Miles, nothing you can say right now is going to help. Let her calm down and then you can have a talk."

"But what's she so upset about? I haven't done anything!"

"Yet. You haven't done anything *yet*. But you will."

Baldwin lets go of my arm. I move over to a large rock and sit down to think. How can I make this right with Gwen when I haven't even done anything?

I lift up a stick and begin randomly picking at the dirt.

I guess I can kind of understand where Gwen's coming from. I mean, I know she likes me. I like her too, of course. So that's why she's mad—no one wants someone they love—I mean, like—to die. But, like I said before, everyone dies.

I keep scribbling aimlessly on the ground.

Still, I can see why actually *knowing* when someone's

going to die can be upsetting, but it's *my* life and *my* death, not hers, and besides, Merlin didn't even say exactly *when* I'm going to die, just *how* I'm going to die. Now let's see, it's going to be my son, and I don't plan on having kids anytime soon, but *if* I do, then he's going to have to get old enough to kill me, so that should be at least…thirty years from now. *At least.*

Two small shoes suddenly come into my field of vision. I look up. It's Gwen. She still looks a little upset, but has stopped crying. She still looks beautiful. She looks beautiful no matter what.

"Nice drawing," she says.

I look down at where I'd been picking at the ground. Apparently I have unconsciously drawn a heart and written Gwen's name in the middle.

"Oh, um, yeah…" I say, standing up in embarrassment. "Listen, Gwen, I—"

"Don't say it, Miles," Gwen interrupts, "It's okay. I overreacted."

"Okay. I really like you. I'll never hurt you."

A half-hearted smile comes over one side of Gwen's mouth. "Yes, you will. But that's okay. We'll figure things out as they come."

"All right. And I'll try not to die anytime soon!" I joke.

Gwen smiles mildly again and takes my hand gently in hers. "Oh, Miles. You really don't understand women, do you?"

Chapter Thirty-Two

We all enjoy, as much as we can, a quiet dinner of tuna fish, crackers, and roasted marshmallows for dessert, but we're so pooped that we don't stay up to tell stories or chat by the fireside. Baldwin's first to go to bed, or go to Buick I should say, cracks a window, and begins snoring almost immediately.

Gwen and I make our way to the tent, set alarms on our phones, and pass out right away, too.

* * * *

I wake up first. I wake up because of the light and heat. It's really bright and quite warm.

"Ugh, what time is it?" I say to myself, squinting and rubbing my eyes.

I check my phone. "1:45! What the heck! Gwen, wake up! We overslept! We're behind schedule!"

Gwen leans up on her elbows, golden hair flowing angelically over her soft shoulders, golden eyes shining brightly from behind heavenly lashes. Even with just having awakened, she looks perfect. But no time to daydream!

"Come on, Gwen. Let's go! No time to waste!"

"What happened? We both set alarms, right?" she asks sleepily.

"Yeah, but they didn't go off," I say, getting packed up as quickly as I can.

"Great. Must be some other enchantment to set us back." Gwen jumps to her feet. "Well, if that's the worst Morgan or whoever can do, they can try all they want and it won't do them any good! Let's go!"

Gwen and I get everything together and start bringing it to the car. No need to have woken Baldwin earlier, but now we're ready to go.

I throw some stuff in the trunk.

"Baldwin! Time to go!" I say, closing the trunk with a thud. I put Archimedes and his terrarium back into the backseat. He spent the night in the tent right by my side, of course. He earned it.

I move around to the driver's side to take first shift. Baldwin's not there, even though I think that's where he fell asleep. I look inside the car, but he's not there. I look around the campsite. He's nowhere to be found.

"Baldwin's missing!" I yell as Gwen comes over to the car.

"What? How? Where could he have gone?"

"I—"

But before I can answer that I have no idea, I see Baldwin come moseying out of the woods, adjusting his pants.

"Baldwin! What the heck! Where were you?" I yell, still in near-panic mode.

Baldwin stops short, looking entirely perplexed that I would ask such a question.

"I went to the bathroom and to change back into my clothes, my Lord. Here, here are yours," he says, handing me a neatly folded stack of the clothes I'd lent him last night.

"Jeez Louise! Tell someone next time, will ya? I nearly had a heart attack!" I say.

"Yes, my Lord."

"All right, well, everyone's here, everyone's ready now? Okay, let's go. I'll drive first." I hop in the driver's seat. Gwen sits next to me and Baldwin's in back. We hit the road.

The plan to make it to Wyoming in a day and a half is still going well despite our morning—well, afternoon—setback. At least now we know not to rely on technology. Apparently it's really prone to enchantment.

"You know," Gwen says out of nowhere after I've been driving for a few hours, "I was thinking, our phones are probably not good to keep around. I mean, none of our enemies even need to use enchantment to mess with us through our phones."

Huh. It's like Gwen can read my mind.

"What do you mean?" Baldwin asks. Apparently he's not on the same wavelength.

"I *mean* that our enemy doesn't even need to use magic to use our phones against us. Anyone who's even remotely good with computers can hack into our phones or pinpoint our exact location using the GPS built in. That's probably how that dragon got to us and how our alarms got turned off."

Baldwin looks at his phone as if he can't believe it.

"Okay, well we need a map first, then we can dump our phones. We'll get one at the next exit," I say.

We pull off at some random exit in South Dakota. The sign says there's a gas stating just 0.7 miles up the road.

We drive for what seems like at least two miles without seeing a thing.

"Where is this place?" I ask, looking at the desolate landscape surrounding us. There really seems to be nothing for miles. Just flat, endless prairie of dead or dying grass. Nothing.

"I don't like this. Let's get back on the highway," Gwen says nervously.

"Okay," I agree.

I turn the car around and head back the way we came. We drive for two miles, three, four.

"Did I miss the highway? I didn't see the on ramp," I say nervously.

"I didn't see it either," Gwen says in a near whisper.

"Maybe we should circle back," Baldwin suggests.

"No. We didn't pass it. And the best course of action when lost is to travel in a straight line," I say.

So we do. No one else has a better plan. We drive and drive and drive on this seemingly abandoned road. Not a single car passes. Not another car comes up from behind and we don't approach any, either. Nothing changes for an hour.

I finally pull onto the dirt shoulder and put the car in park, but I don't turn it off for fear that whatever enchantment is cast over us right now may prevent the car from starting again.

"Okay, this isn't working. We have to try something

else," I say. Gwen's busy messing around on her phone. She's been doing so the whole time we've been lost.

"Well, I have no idea where we are. My GPS is jammed and I can't call, text, or do anything at all. I knew these things would only bring us trouble," she says, finally dropping her phone to her lap in frustration.

"Well we have to try something," I say.

"What's that?" Baldwin says, pointing at something out on the horizon.

"What?" I ask, looking where he's pointing but seeing nothing.

"There. You see it? That glint out there in the field. Something shiny."

I squint to try and make out what he's talking about. Then I see it. Something *is* shining out there, but what, I can't tell.

"Maybe it's that gas station. Or at least some type of building. Hopefully someone there can tell us where we are," Gwen says.

"Okay, I'll go check it out," I say.

"No! You can't go alone!" Gwen says, grabbing me by the arm. "What if it's a trap?"

"Well we can't all go. Someone should stay with the car," I say.

"I'll go," Baldwin says semi-confidently. "I already fought in a battle once!" He chuckles nervously. "You stay here with Gwen. I'll be fine."

I don't like the idea of Baldwin going out there alone, but I like the idea of leaving Gwen alone even less.

"All right. I'll even let you take Excalibur, just in case! Let me get it," I say. I get out of the car and open the back door to get Excalibur. Baldwin and Gwen are talking quietly. Gwen's probably telling him to be careful and safe and come back quick if anything looks suspicious. She's such a great girl.

I grab Excalibur and shut the back door. I hear a click like the doors locked, but it sounds extra forceful. Weird. I try to open the door to check, but it's locked.

I move around to Gwen's door. Also locked. I tell her to open it. She tries, but the lock won't budge and neither will the door. She looks scared.

I walk around to the back on the opposite side of where Baldwin's sitting.

"Cover your head!" I yell, but Gwen's already put her head between her knees and Baldwin's already leaning to the side, covering Archimedes' terrarium with his body, both having realized what I plan to do next.

I line up Excalibur's blade with the door window. I raise the sword with both hands and bring it crashing down against the window—CLANG! My arms recoil as if I struck a wall of titanium. I look at the glass—not a scratch.

Baldwin, Gwen, and Archimedes are trapped and I'm all alone on the outside, in the middle of an enchanted nowhere.

Chapter Thirty-Three

What to do? What to do? I can't break my friends out of the car and they can't get out from the inside. It's like there's a force field built into the car that we can't control that's keeping them trapped.

"Miles! Miles!"

I see Gwen's mouth move but I can't hear her voice. Not even a muffled likeness. Great! Apparently the force field even makes the car soundproof!

I run around to the passenger seat where Gwen's sitting. I'm not the best lip reader, but I can make out easy words, especially if people emphasize the words and talk slowly.

"Miles!" Gwen's lips read, "Go find out..." I miss the end of the sentence.

"What? I can't hear you!" I say loudly, shaking my head from side to side and pointing to my ears so she can figure out what I'm saying.

She gets it. I see it in her face.

She moves her lips slowly, emphatically, so I can understand her.

160

C.E. *Zyburo*

"Go…find…out…what…the…thing…out…there…
is…" she says, pointing out to the shiny thing in the
field.

"I can't leave you!" I yell, even though I know she
can't hear me. For some reason I still think it will help her
understand what I'm saying if I yell.

She looks calm, looks as if she's talking quietly now.

"You…have…to…" her lips read. "Get…help. Get…
us…out."

I look down at the sword in my hand. She's right.
She's always right. I have to leave them. I'm obviously no
help standing around here smacking an enchanted car like
a baby with a spoon and a pan.

"Okay," I say to her.

She puts her hand on the window. I place my hand
over the glass on top of hers.

"I…love…you…" she mouths.

I can't believe she just said that, but there's no
mistaking those words, even through a force
field-protected Buick.

"I love you too," I say to her.

She smiles. What a beautiful smile. She leans
forward. I lean over, too, getting right up to the glass.
She's just on the other side. She closes her eyes and
pushes out her lips. I do the same. My lips touch only
glass, but in my mind I can still feel her, still feel what it's
like to meet those perfect lips with my own. And it's more
than my imagination. Somehow, I feel her, feel her in my
body and soul. The force field couldn't block the power of
our first kiss.

I pull back. She's smiling. She looks at me with
adoring eyes.

"Good…luck…" she mouths.

I smile and turn away, walking toward the mysterious glint in the field.

I don't look back.

Chapter Thirty-Four

What is that thing?

I trudge across the seemingly endless prairie wondering what on earth I can be headed for now.

I walk close to half a mile before I can even make out what I'm walking toward—it's a pavilion, a colorful tent of red and gold stripes, that looks like it's set up for a jousting tournament.

But what was that glistening then? There's nothing shiny on the pavilion, nothing that would send a glare bright enough for us to see all the way back on the road.

Then I see what signaled us, and it sends fear all the way through me to my very bones. There's a knight in full armor on horseback hiding—or attempting to hide—behind the pavilion, waiting to ambush whomever happens to venture near. I stop and crouch down in the tall, brown grass, putting Excalibur flat against the earth.

If that knight's armor could send a shining glare all the way to me, then certainly Excalibur could have accidentally signaled him as to my presence. I look back to the road. The Buick's easily in view and even though I'm only halfway between the car and the pavilion, the devious knight must have certainly already noticed me approaching.

I make a split decision and jump back onto my feet, dusting myself off and swearing, kicking the ground. I'm acting like I tripped in the hope that the knight won't realize I noticed him hiding. I put my hand over my eyes and squint at the pavilion. I see the knight retreat fully back behind it.

Good. I think he bought it.

I continue marching toward the death trap, slowing my pace as much as possible to buy myself some time to strategize but not so slow as to draw suspicion.

I have about half a mile to plan, about five minutes. All right, so, the knight must be an enemy of mine. I'm obviously going to have to fight him and hope that breaks the spell keeping my friends captive in the Buick. He's on horseback and is in full armor—an obvious advantage for him, but there's nothing I can do about that. I only have my sword and am on foot, but I do have one advantage—surprise. He thinks the element of surprise is on his side, but *I* know that he's hiding and I know *where* he is, so truthfully that'll work against him. Now, how to use this to my best advantage…

I keep walking calmly and steadily toward the pavilion as I continue to formulate my plan. I think I've gotten it figured out as best as I can.

When I'm a few hundred feet away, I fall to the ground with a loud thud.

"Oh! Oh! My leg! Ah! Help me! Please, someone, help me!" I scream.

No one answers. I'm lying as flat as I can with the ground and can't see the pavilion. I can't see anything but grass, but I'm working as quickly yet as quietly as I can in the dirt.

"Ow! Please! Oh, it hurts! Please, is someone there? Please, if anyone can hear me, please help!" I yell as loud as I can, working diligently as I scream.

A few moments of silence, and finally I hear a reply.

"Who is there? Identify yourself!" comes a deep, loathsome, unsure voice from the direction of the pavilion.

"I'm just a kid! I think I fell in a gopher hole or something! Help me, please!" I'm almost done...

No answer for a time, then the dangerous voice calls out again.

"Who are you?"

"My name is Miles. Miles Arthur! I'm a long way from home and my friends are trapped. Please, we need help!"

"Stand up and I will come help you!"

"I can't! I, I think it's broken! Please! Help me!"

"Show me where you are and I will come to your aid!"

Perfect timing. I've just finished. I stick Excalibur into the dirt behind me. The long sword towers over the prairie grass.

"Here! I'm here! Thank you, sir! Oh, thank you! Come quick!" I begin to scurry away from Excalibur and the pavilion at a slight angle, staying extremely low, moving slowly, and staying within dirt patches free of grass as much as possible. The going's tedious, but in a very short time I begin to hear the sound I'd hoped for—galloping hooves.

I'm about ten feet away from Excalibur when the ground really begins to tremble, the vibrations growing stronger and stronger as the knight brings his horse to full speed and charges ever closer.

I stop and turn my body around to face Excalibur. I hide myself as much as possible in the brown grass.

The earth really begins to quake and I see the enemy knight in his perfectly shined, glistening armor riding fiercely toward Excalibur. He lowers the lance he's carrying directly at my blade, and as soon as he reaches his target, aims to strike. But I'm not there and he notices my trap too late. His horse trips in the deep pit I was able to dig with my sword and hands as I distracted him with my screaming lie of having been injured. The knight flies straight forward off of his horse and his lance sticks in the dirt to his right. Lucky guess by me, hoping for him to be right-handed, otherwise I would be a shish kabob right now. But there's no time to celebrate just yet. Before the knight can recover, I need to get Excalibur and bring my enemy down!

I jump up from my hiding spot and run to grab my sword. Unfortunately for me, my adversary is well-trained, because as soon as I pull Excalibur from the earth, the knight is already on his feet and drawing his sword.

"Very clever, you little rat!" the knight says evilly from under his helm. His face is fully covered. I can't even see his eyes through the two narrow slits through which he can apparently view me.

"We don't have to fight, you know," I say as we begin circling each other, swords out, ready for battle.

"Oh, but we must. Yes, we really must!"

C.E. Zyburo

The knight makes the first move, striking ferociously at my neck. I block, but his blow is strong. He's much stronger than me. Not good.

"Why? Why must we fight?" I ask, thrusting at him with less than full force. He slams my sword out of the way easily.

"Why? Why?" He charges at me with his body. I step to the side and knock away his sword as he passes by. "Because you claim kingship, but no illegitimate *boy* will be my king!"

He slices low before we have even returned to our fighting stance. Not what I expected from such a seemingly well-trained warrior. He nearly catches me off my guard, but I'm able to block just in time. That was close! All right, no more messing around!

I begin my attack, making a strike with every word I speak,

"I"—CLANG!—"Claim"—CLANG!—"nothing!"—CLA NG! All of my strikes are blocked.

The knight laughs. "Arthur, you claimed your throne when you claimed that sword. Only the King can use Excalibur!"

He thrusts, I block. I'm sweating terribly. I'm getting tired. *Definitely* not good.

"King of what? I don't even know what I'm king of!" I yell and begin my counterattack.

Our blows are evenly matched until a quick, slicing stroke of mine catches the knight's shoulder, but his armor is strong and my blade glances off.

"Whomever wields Excalibur is the king of all! And once I kill you and take it, *I* will be king!"

The knight seems energized by the thought and

comes at me with extra force. It's all I can do to prevent him from slicing me in two. But when the last, violent swing of his sword meets my defensive block, the unthinkable happens—Excalibur slips from my sweaty palms and is flung high into the air and far away, getting lost among the grass.

"Haha!" the knight laughs cynically. "You see? Noble blood may destine you for kingship, but it doesn't destine you to *live*, and what good is kingship without life? Let's see how noble your blood really is."

The knight comes at me. I back away slowly in fear. I could yield, I could beg for mercy, but I doubt it'll do me any good. This knight wants to kill me, and he will.

He thrusts at my chest, and I jump out of the way, but not fast enough. His blade cuts into my right arm, halfway between my shoulder and elbow. I feel my warm, sticky blood begin to flow.

"Oh, Arthur. Not such a valiant death after all. Unarmed, no armor!"

He strikes again, this time at my leg, making a sweeping downward strike that makes a horrible gash on my left thigh. He's just toying with me, like a sadistic cat playing with a mouse that has no chance of escape. He could kill me with one blow, but he wants to taunt me first. He wants to make me suffer.

I'm getting light-headed from the fight and loss of blood. I'm running out of time. I have to do something.

"Okay, Nameless Knight. You may not consider this a valiant death, but for you it's certainly not a valiant kill. You may become king, but the manner in which you become king will be forever tarnished by the cowardly way in which you killed me here today."

The knight seems to look at me from the black void behind his helm.

"Cowardly, say you? I suppose you would have me arm you to make this a fair fight. Should I give you armor and food as well? Perhaps time to recover from your wounds? Do you take me for a fool, Arthur? In war, death comes bitterly to all who meet the blade!"

"Then do it quickly!" I command.

"Now *that* I can do!"

The knight makes his death thrust directly at my stomach. When the point is just about to pierce my body and make a mess of my internal organs, I lunge to the right with my right arm extended and grab the knight's hand where he's gripping his sword, trying to pull him close to me using his own inertia against him. But the knight is an experienced swordsman. With his blade under my left arm where I'm trying to pull him through, instead of stumbling forward he pushes the blade into my side. He doesn't have enough force to cut into me at such an awkward angle, so I put my left arm down in an attempt to trap his blade. But he's quick-thinking and ruthless. He twists the blade, peeling away at the inside of my arm and the side of my ribcage at the same time.

"AHHH!" I scream, but almost instinctually realize I can use nearly the same move that won me my first victory against Kay.

I drop to the ground, still clinging to my enemy's sword with all my strength, even though it hurts tremendously. I kick the knight's feet out from under him. He is overweighed with his armor and hits the ground hard, losing his grip on his sword as he tumbles and as it sticks tightly into my body.

I don't have time to worry about my injuries. I stand quickly, readying the defiled sword dripping with my own blood. I stand over the Nameless Knight, sword aimed just below his helm and above his chest plate at the narrow opening revealing his neck. I thrust the sword home without a second thought and immediately pass out.

C.E. Zyburo

Chapter Thirty-Five

Dim light growing ever brighter. Incoherent mumbling.
No, words. They *are* words. The light gets brighter. I see
a face. Beautiful Gwen, my angel.

"Miles! Miles! Are you awake?" she cries. She looks
lovely but seems to have been crying.

"Wha- what? What happened?"

"Baldwin! He's waking up!" she calls over her
shoulder, then turning back to me, "Miles! Thank God!
You've been out for two days!"

"Two days? Where am I?" I certainly feel groggy for
having just woken up from a two-day sleep. Well, I guess
being unconscious isn't the same as sleeping.

Baldwin comes into view beside Gwen, looking
down at me where I'm lying.

"My King! You've come back to us! Merlin assured
us that you would!"

"Merlin's here?" I ask, sitting up in earnestness to see
him. But the excruciating pain in my side forces me back
down.

"He was. He's gone now. We found him tending to you in the field once the Buick unlocked."

Now the memory starts coming back to me. I fought a Nameless Knight to the death, but fainted immediately after killing him due to exhaustion and blood loss.

"So I did win," I sigh, the victory not feeling as amazing as it should. I feel no pride in it at all, actually. "And what of the Nameless Knight?"

"Gone. Just his armor was left. Just like the knights who attacked your house," Baldwin explains.

Good. I don't want to kill anyone. But sending a conjured body out of existence is fine by me.

"So we're still in South Dakota? We haven't made any progress in two days?" I'm worried. Time's running dangerously short.

"No. We couldn't move you. Merlin warned us not to. Your wounds were too severe and we couldn't take you to the hospital or they would have called all our parents and sent us straight home. Lucky for you not all of Merlin's learning is in magic. He also knows a great deal about medicine. Mostly ancient, natural cures, of course, but you're alive! It worked!" Baldwin leans over and gives me a tremendous hug. In addition to my side, my arm hurts where he embraces me and my leg feels like it's on fire where his body presses down.

"Unhh…" I groan in pain.

"Oh, sorry!" Baldwin jumps up, realizing he's hurting me. "Just so excited that you're alive and well, my Liege."

"Alive, yes. Well? Not so much," I say with a chuckle.

I look to Gwen who's standing quietly in the corner.

Then I realize the place we're in. It looks like the inside of the Nameless Knight's pavilion. It's big enough for all of us to sit, lay down, move around. Plenty of room for more, too.

Suddenly I hear two voices and the sound of heavy boots on the ground coming toward us. I'm startled. I look around quickly for Excalibur. I don't see it.

"Baldwin! Quick! Get Excalibur!" I yell, jumping to my feet despite the anguish my injuries send firing through my entire body.

But there's no time to arm myself. The two knights are at the entrance to the pavilion. I stand still as a statue, prepared to fight with my bare hands if necessary.

"And tat's why ya should never wear chainmail ta a swimming 'ole!" one of the knights says.

The other bursts out laughing. "Haha! Good one, Ban!"

They both turn to me at the same time. They're holding a dead deer upside down tied by its legs to a stick they're carrying over their shoulders.

"Hullo! What's t'is? Normally tis ta knights 'oo salute ta king and not ta other way round!" says the knight in back, pointing below my waist.

The other laughs hysterically, then says, "Bors! Is tat anyway ta greet ye king?"

I look down. I'm stark naked.

Baldwin comes up and throws a robe around me quickly.

"Apologies, my King. I should have told you about our new friends. This is Ban," he points to the knight in front, who nods his head, "And his brother, Bors," the one in back nods, "Allies who have come to help us."

Gwen comes over to me. "Sit down, Miles. You shouldn't over-exert yourself."

I follow her guiding hands and take a seat on my cot.

"Ban and Bors? What kind of names are those?" I say, trying to recuperate from my embarrassment by throwing out an insult.

"Ay? As good as Miles Art'ur, I s'pose," says Ban, getting to work skinning the deer while his brother Bors assists.

I shoot an angry glance at Ban but he's too busy to notice.

"Okay, Ban and Bors," I say, "You've come to help, have you? And how do you propose to do that? The car's full. We can't take you along with us."

"Oh, ta car, eh? Ya still plan on takin' tat 'unk o' enchanted junk to find ta Lady o' ta Lake, do ya now?" says Bors, cutting up some deer meat.

Baldwin leans over to me and whispers, "My Lord, we torched our phones and the Buick while you were recuperating. We couldn't risk another trap."

I look at him in shock. "No car? Then how are we going to get to Wyoming?"

Ban looks at me with a big grin on his face. "Ta good ol' fashion way, my King—on 'orse!"

I nearly faint at the news.

On a horse? I don't even know how to *ride* a horse, let alone travel cross country on one.

I feel a strong hand on my shoulder. I look up. It's either Ban or Bors. I can't tell now they've switched positions. They look exactly the same—tall, well-built, young, probably around my age, but with a look of age and experience I'll probably never have. Their shoulder-length thick and wavy chestnut hair make them look like ancient Greek warriors. The fact that they're clad in full medieval-style armor doesn't hurt, either.

"My King, I t'ink we got off on ta wrong foot," he says soothingly in his odd accent, mature enough to extend the olive branch first. "My brother an' I love ta joke. 'Tis our nature. If we tidn't laugh, we'd cry! Now, if ya'd like, I'd be glad ta explain ta situation we all find ourselves in—currently."

I stand to meet this ally of mine eye to eye, but I find myself short by at least half a foot. I guess face to tilted face will have to do.

"All right. Please *do* explain. And try to do a little better job than Merlin."

I offer my hand. He takes it firmly in his.

"Haha! Tat ol' sorcerer t'inks he knows everything, but he certainly don't know 'ow ta tell a tale! Let us walk."

He turns and walks out of the tent. I guess I'm supposed to follow, even though I'm in a robe and shoeless.

I turn to Baldwin and mouth, "Bors?"

He shakes his head. "Ban," he mouths back.

I nod and walk out of the pavilion to have my conversation with Ban.

Chapter Thirty-Six

"So, what t'ya want ta know?" Ban asks, walking patiently beside me to match my gait that's slowed considerably because of my injuries.

"Well, everything, really. Merlin said I'm a reincarnated King Arthur, Gwen is Guinevere, and the Ectors are reincarnated, too. But those people, well, us, in the past, were all nobles in England. We're not in England, so what the heck am I king of?"

Ban looks off over the endlessly rolling plains. We're walking along a road in ill-repair—the grass is invading from the sides and springing up through cracks in the pavement. It looks similar to the place I last remember being before I went unconscious for two days—the enchanted road that never ended, only now there's an obvious absence of magic. There's no feeling of anxiety, no feeling of enchantment. I feel safe.

Ban extends his arm, pointing to nothing in particular, pointing to everything. "You are king ta all o' tis and more. But 'tis not land ta which ye are entitled.

No, land 'as not been ta source o' power for many a year. Ya see, in medieval England, ta more land ye controlled, ta more power ya had. But 'tis not ta case anymore. You, Sire, are king o' ta people. Ye will bring magic once again into tis world, and ta people will love ye and follow ya for it!"

"How? I don't know any magic."

Ban laughs. "'Tis all 'round ya! Now I know Merlin told ya at least tat much! D'ya t'ink tat dragon 'oo attacked ye just spends 'is time in someone's back yard? D'ya t'ink ta knights tat attacked ye at Bedgrayne jus' come an' go as t'ey please? Apologies for 'avin' missed tat battle, by ta way. Jus' goes ta show ye tat 'istory tain't doomed ta repeat 'erself, tis jus' tat she sometimes does, 'tis all. But no, my King, 'tis magic all 'round tat keeps t'ese t'ings 'idden from ta world taday, but t'ey are startin' ta reappear, for ta king 'as returned!"

"So just my being born has brought back all this evil? Evil knights and evil dragons? Better I'd not been reincarnated, then..."

What a drag. My life only brings evil...

"Not so! No, not so 't'all!" Ban grabs me by my shoulders and looks at me with a stern tenderness. "Ya 'ave met wit ta evil, but 'tis only ta beginnin'! Ta first time ye became king, in medieval times, ye was met wit plenty o' evil as well, but ye overcame it all and ta reign o' King Arthur was more peaceful t'an any before o' since! 'Twill be ta same again, my Lord."

"Okay," I say, turning to walk on. That makes me feel a little better. "So I will make peace for the world? Is that what you're telling me? I'll be responsible for world peace?"

Ban smiles. "In a way. T'ere will always be enemies to ta peace, my Lord, like tat sister o' yourn, for instance." Ban spits on the ground at having to even mention her, "But yes, 'tis ye destiny to bring a time o' tranquility to ta world."

Well, I can deal with that. That sounds really good, actually. I could use some tranquility after my pains and adventures.

"How? How can I do that when no one even knows my name? I'm not famous. I'm not a leader."

"O' course ya are! Ya rounded up a bunch o' sissy high school lads ta fight a dark army! Ya battled an unknown knight when ya were drastically outmatched! T'ese deeds, an' many more, will make ye known ta world 'round."

"I guess I'll have to take your word for it," I say awkwardly, still not quite believing everything Ban is telling me.

"Humility tain't a bad trait, my Lord, but ye should not shy away from accomplishments."

I try to hide my smile. "Tell me more about this magic, the magic in the world. How has it been gone for so long? How has no one found out about it, stumbled upon it, or used it for so long? I mean, we've come so far with science and everything since the Middle Ages, how have we not discovered—or re-discovered—this stuff?"

"In some ways, people 'ave discovered an' made use o' magic, but magic an' science do not go 'and 'n 'and. In many a way, t'ey fight each ot'er, t'ey contradict one anot'er, an' for centuries science has won tat battle. But many are starting ta understand and many more will once ta king becomes known to ta world. T'ink about quantum physics if ya will. D'ya know much about ta subject?"

"I, uh… no, not really."

"Well, 'tis a science tat is getting' close to ta realm o' magic. Ya see, t'ere's a t'eory which states tat a particle, like an electron in a atom, is on'y located at a specific position *because* one is lookin' for it. Tis ta act o' lookin' which makes ta electron be where 'tis. T'ya understand?"

"Uh…"

"'Tis like losin' somethin' an' findin' it somewhere it shouldn't be, but in actuality, 'tis exactly where it should be because ye looked for it t'ere. Magic tis ta same. 'T'as been gone for centuries because no one was lookin' for it!"

"Well, some people have. Merlin has and apparently so have some enemies of mine."

"Quite true. And t'ere are ot'ers as well. And twill be many more in ta years ta come."

"Is that where you come from? Some magic world?"

I consider Ban's strong physique, the other-worldly way in which he carries himself, his outlandish accent. He must be from some magic realm.

"Me? Why, certainly I come from a magic land. 'Tis called Ireland!" Ban laughs and smacks me, rather too roughly, on the back. "My Lord, I t'ink ye a bit confused still. T'ere's no 'magic worlds.' Our world 'as all ta magic ye o' anyone else will ever need! 'Tis waking up is all tat magic needs, o' rather, 'tis ta people tat need ta waking."

Ban tilts his head, telling me to look to the right. I do and see we're back at the pavilion, even though we've been walking in a straight line along the road away from the campsite for some time now. The smell of cooked venison is permeating the air.

I spin around, trying to figure out where we'd walked to, where we'd just come from.

"What? I, I don't remember turning around to come back—"

Ban laughs loudly and deeply. "Haha! 'Tis just an ol' parlor trick! Somet'in ta use on ye friends, particularly after a few drinks! Always gets 'em!"

Ban slaps my back again. I don't think I'll ever get used to his humor or his strength.

"Just a bit o' fun, my Lord. Only magic I know, if ye can even call it tat. Per'aps I'll teach it t'ya one day. Now, let us go get some o' tat fine venison Bors 'as been cookin'!"

Ban trots off into the tent as happy as can be. I follow slowly, nursing my wounds, my back being the sorest of all.

Chapter Thirty-Seven

Ban and Bors do most of the talking over our dinner of grilled venison and boiled field greens. They tell us stories of battles they've fought, always seeming to disagree over who did what, who led the charge, who drew the final stroke. But it's all in good fun. The twins hardly ever stop laughing.

"So, we'll be on our way tomorrow, then?" I ask, helping to clean up after the meal.

Ban and Bors are busy cutting up, drying, and salting the rest of the deer, which isn't much since they both eat as much as lions.

"O' course. Got ta meet ta Lady o' ta Lake by ta fourteenth o' October, ain't tat so?" says Bors, not even pausing to look up from his work.

"Well, actually, we need to have the scabbard to Mr., er, Sir Ector by that date," Baldwin explains nervously, looking down at his twiddling thumbs.

Both Ban and Bors stop their work and stare at Baldwin upon hearing this.

"What?" says Ban angrily. "Ye said we 'ad til ta fourteenth ta get ta scabbard. Ye said nuttin' about getting' it nowhere else."

"Well, I…yes, but…" Baldwin stalls nervously.

"He said that because Miles needed his rest. He needed to recover from his injuries. We couldn't drag him along in his condition," Gwen says firmly, a visible fire behind her eyes.

Ban and Bors look at each other. They lean close together and mumble to each other for some time, having a private conversation no one else can make out.

Ban stands up after a few minutes. "All right t'en, we 'ad better get a move on."

"What, tonight?" Baldwin asks.

"We 'ave no choice," Ban says, looking sternly at Baldwin until he drops his gaze.

"Then let's get ready," Gwen says, starting to pack up our things.

I do what I can packing up alongside Baldwin. Ban and Bors take care of the venison and their own things. We all work silently. We're all worried about making it to the Lady of the Lake within our allotted timeframe while also leaving time to travel back to wherever Dad happens to be to to get him the scabbard in time to save his life. Oh yeah, that's another thing I have to worry about—actually finding my father. He's off somewhere guarding the president, but where? He could be anywhere in the world. I guess I'll worry about crossing that bridge when I come to it.

"Time ta 'ead out!" Ban yells from the front of a line of five magnificent horses and a sturdy-looking mule he and his brother apparently brought with them. The sun set

C.E. Zyburo

about an hour ago, but the dark night apparently won't slow Ban down. He hops up onto his great, grey steed, making it look as easy as can be. Bors follows suit, jumping on the second grey horse. I finish strapping Archimedes to the pack mule at the back of the line, which is loaded down with all sorts of supplies saved from the torched Buick as well as what Ban and Bors have brought—though they appear to travel light—then move to the fourth horse, a medium-sized brown mare, to help Gwen up. I move to the horse in back, but Baldwin stops me.

"No, my King. You ride in the middle, the safest place. I'll bring up the rear."

"All right. Just keep an eye on Archimedes for me," I say.

"Yes, my Lord."

Baldwin gives me a boost onto my black beast of a horse. I feel like I'm ten feet in the air. Baldwin takes his spot and grabs a rope to lead the mule. We get on our way.

"Say, what are the names of these fine animals?" I call ahead to Ban and Bors. We might as well kill some time in conversation. We have a long ride ahead.

"Phil, Bill, Jelly, Betsy, Larry, and Terry," Bors replies.

"Really? Those don't sound like war horse names," I say.

"No? Tat's because t'ey named after me favorite sandwiches—ta good ol' PB and J an' ta infamous BLT! Haha!" Bors laughs so hard he nearly falls off Bill.

We all chuckle. I guess they're as good of names as any.

"Good, Jelly. Good boy," I whisper in Jelly's ear, rubbing his neck. He gives a short snort of approval.

I look behind me and Gwen and Baldwin are bonding with their horses as well. Good. The tension's easing.

* * * *

The going's slow during the whole night since the horses aren't used to travelling in the dark, but since we have flashlights, or "torches" as Ban and Bors call them, we don't stop, not even to eat, until the sun begins to rise.

"Time for brunch!" Ban calls out.

Finally! We're all so hungry we don't mind Ban calling this early morning meal brunch. We hop off our horses, all of which immediately begin to "brunch" themselves, grazing on the ample grass which is now a lush green. We must have left the brown prairies behind us during the night.

Everyone scarfs down a hearty meal of venison and baked beans. Not the best breakfast I've ever had, but under the circumstances, it's delicious.

After feeding Archimedes, I rub some of the ancient medicinal ointment Merlin left for me on my wounds, which are healing quickly. The scar tissue's already forming in some places, my flesh turning a soft purplish-pink, a very good sign.

"'*Courage alone can only be shown, with bodily scars to be forever known,*'" I mumble to myself, remembering the second token needed for the Lady of the Lake. Well, at least two parts of the triple quest are completed.

"You look much better," Gwen says, sitting down

next to me. "When we found you on that field... I don't even want to think about it!"

I take Gwen's hand in mine. "I'm fine. Thanks for taking care of me."

She smiles softly and squeezes my hand.

"You're welcome."

Her golden eyes reflect the blazing colors of the sunrise perfectly. This girl is amazing. She's so lovely. I start leaning into her, hoping to have our second kiss, our first one without force field-protected glass between our lips.

"Time ta be on our way, lovebirds!" Ban yells, way too loudly for it being so early in the morning. He pulls his head back from where he stuck it in between Gwen's and mine and trots over to round up the horses.

Gwen squeezes my hand one more time and gets up to go.

"Guess these guys don't sleep," she says, and hurries toward Betsy as if she doesn't need any rest, either.

I hop onto Jelly and turn back to Baldwin, who also has way more pep in his step than he should at this hour, especially after such a long night of travelling.

"All right, guys, what's going on? How do you all have so much energy? I'm pooped and can hardly move another inch!" I say.

Everyone looks around at each other in a suspicious manner, like they know something I don't. Suddenly, Ban and Bors burst out laughing.

"Okay, okay. Ye made it pretty far. Just 'ad ta test ta strength o' ta new king, is all!" Ban says, dismounting and walking over to me with a large, old, leather flask. "Try t'is. Will take all ta weariness out o' ye limbs."

I take a small swig from the canteen, not knowing what to expect. The taste is awful and the liquid burns all the way down my throat and into my stomach.

"AGH!" I choke out, nearly vomiting and almost dropping the flask. Ban grabs it from my shaking hand and laughs heartily.

"Haha! 'Tis good all ta way down!"

He walks back to his horse and starts the line moving, our horses following the one ahead like the well-trained animals that they are.

I'm still slumped over in my saddle from the awful burning in my insides that's spread all throughout my body, but as the fire slowly dies down, it's replaced with what I can only describe as an energizing effect. It feels like every muscle, every nerve, every cell in my body is just bursting with energy. Not jittery energy like from caffeine, just pure, unadulterated stimulation.

"Whoa! I feel great!" I call out.

"Haha! We t'ought ya might! Even ta horses approve o' Merlin's Enchanted Energizer!"

Chapter Thirty-Eight

"So how long do the effects last?" I ask, wondering how long such a fantastically energizing potion can possibly work.

"Well, 'tisn't recommended ta take it more t'an t'ree days in a row. More t'an t'ree days wit'out sleep and one begins ta hallucinate!" Bors explains.

"Well, hopefully we can make it to Yellowstone in three days or less!" I say, knowing that our travel will now be much slower than we'd initially planned. Nonetheless, even with having to completely discard our original timeline, we still have nearly a week to finish our quest. I know it's possible. It's *got* to be possible.

"'Twill take closer ta six days jus' ta get t'ere. We will 'ave ta take t'ree days o' travel, a day o' rest, an' anot'er two days ta make it ta rest o' ta way. 'Twill be close, but tis possible," Ban says.

"I guess that's the best that can be hoped for," I reply.

* * * *

And it is. The first three days and nights that follow are full of nothing but travelling on horseback, but I must say, Jelly and the rest of the horses are doing most of the work and they don't complain a bit. Their strength and endurance give us the same.

The flat grasslands eventually begin to be spotted here and there with trees until the landscape is full of them and we're surrounded by dense forests. We take our day of rest and all of us sleep for an entire twenty-four hours. We get up, take some long swigs of Merlin's Energizer, and begin the final leg of our journey. We are all in high spirits on the outside, but I know that I, at least, am feeling a dreadful sense that time's running short, and fast.

The day is once again full of nonstop travelling, save for the occasional meal break which only comes twice every twenty-four hours. But eventually, finally, we begin to reach the small outcroppings of the Rocky Mountains. We've made it to Wyoming!

Ban has been leading us using a topographical map and matching it to the surrounding landscape. I must say, he's been doing an excellent job, but now we have paused on our trek and he appears a bit confused.

"Is something wrong?" Gwen asks, thinking the same thing as me.

"Uh, not'in' ta worry about, missuhs, I mean, ya Grace," Ban says with a touch of nervousness in his voice that he can't conceal. He's studying the map intensely. I notice that Bors has his hand on the hilt of his sword and is taking in his surroundings, studying them intently. He appears to be looking for something, searching the woods

C.E. Zyburo

for some unseen danger. My hand moves instinctively to the hilt of Excalibur.

Just in time, too, because immediately and without the slightest notice, without the ruffle of a leaf, a figure comes bursting out of the trees to our left. I draw my sword, as do Ban and Bors, but the shape moves like a shadow and doesn't stop. It simply dashes through the hundred-foot or so gap in between my horse and Bors' as quick as lightning and then disappears into the trees on our right.

"What the heck was that?" Baldwin calls out.

"I don't know, but I'm going to find out," I say, jumping down from Jelly to pursue the mystery on foot. The forest to the right is too dense and full of undergrowth to risk venturing in with our horses, so I've got to go on foot.

"And I will go wit' ye," says Bors, running over next to me. "O' are ye a skilled tracker, particularly in t'ese unfamiliar lands?"

"Good point," I say.

"I'm going too," says Gwen, dismounting in a surprisingly graceful manner.

No use arguing, I already know that, so I just nod in agreement.

"Aw, man. I never get to do anything!" Baldwin pouts.

"Oh, quit ye whining! Ya sound like a child!" Bors says.

"Besides, ye get ta spend time wit' good ol' Ban!" Ban says, tying up the horses. "May as well 'ave a bit o' grub while ta adventurers are off, mightn't we?"

"Oh, well… in that case," Baldwin says happily.

189

"Ha! Typical! Ma always said the way to a man's heart is through his stomach," Gwen jokes.

"Oh, yeah? I haven't seen you doin' any cookin' for *me*," I say with a smile.

Gwen slugs me playfully on the arm.

"Ya know, we tain't a have no luck trackin' wit' ye dodo, I mean, *lovebirds*, makin' such a racket!" Bors scolds.

"Oh, sorry," Gwen and I apologize sheepishly, but as we make our way as silently as possible into the northern woods, I can see Bors smiling like a happy schoolchild who just pulled one over on his teacher.

Bors checks every leaf and twig that juts out further than the others in the direction in which we last saw the figure moving. He gets low to the ground and checks the dirt for prints every now and then as well. We move in a fairly straight line for about a quarter of a mile, and then we hear something.

Bors stands as straight and still as a lamp post, signaling with his hand for Gwen and I to do the same. He takes a couple of slow, cautious steps forward, peering around a tree. Gwen and I wait about ten feet behind, holding our breaths. I have Excalibur at the ready and Gwen has a short blade in her hand in case even she should need to defend herself. After a few tense moments, Bors turns away from the tree and walks quietly over to Gwen and I.

"Good t'ing ye came along, me lady. Appears ta be a lady's business," he whispers.

"What do you mean?" Gwen asks.

"Go an' 'ave a look. But quiet, now," he says.

Gwen walks over to the tree and peers around as Bors

had. It only takes a second for her to drop her blade quietly to the ground and disappear around the tree.

I start walking toward where she disappeared, but Bors grabs my arm to halt me.

"What? What is it?" I ask.

"Tis just a young lass, no older t'an ten, cryin' by a crude cross in ta ground."

Chapter Thirty-Nine

Several minutes go by and nothing happens. There are no sounds and there's no movement in these woods. Even the wind is silent. Bors and I stare at the trees, at the little slivers of sky we can just make out beyond the thick canopy of leaves. We even stare at our own two feet when there's nothing left to look at or ponder.

"We're wasting time. I'm going to get Gwen," I say impatiently, and march toward the tree she disappeared behind.

But even as I reach the thick, aged trunk, I slow my step and just peek around. Bors is behind me, peeking over my shoulder.

I see Gwen kneeling next to the little girl, talking to her softly, comforting her. They're huddled together in front of a cross made from two large branches of oak tied together in the middle with some large rope. The little girl is wearing a dirty grey, hooded cloak covering her from head to toe. It looks like something an old monk would wear. I guess that's why we couldn't tell what she was when she darted past us earlier.

Gwen looks up from where she's kneeling and catches my eye. Bors and I pull back behind the tree, feeling like peeping Toms who have just been caught spying.

"It's all right, boys. Come on out," Gwen calls.

Bors and I walk out from behind the tree reluctantly. We approach the girls. I can tell they have both been crying, but they seem okay now.

"These are two of the friends I was telling you about. This is Bors, and this is Miles." Gwen introduces us to the little girl. We nod, still a bit embarrassed. "This is Grace."

Grace stands and makes a sweet curtsey.

"Are you really the King?" she asks me, full of wide-eyed wonder, her innocent, dark brown eyes contrasting greatly with her blonde hair that's so light it appears nearly colorless.

"I...I suppose so," I say, even more embarrassed than before.

Grace stares at me with such awe that I'm forced to look away. I don't deserve such reverence, especially from a little girl I just met.

"This is where Grace comes to remember her mother, who died only a year ago," Gwen explains solemnly.

"Oh, deepest apologies, young lass. 'Tis a beautiful place for eternal rest, be it any consolation," Bors says.

"She's not buried here. Father wouldn't let me bury her. If he knew I even made this memorial, he'd punish me horribly!" Grace cries, nearly bursting into tears at the thought of it. Even I have to hold back my sorrow. The poor girl looks so distraught it's heartbreaking.

"Father's a monster. But that will all change now that

real knights and even the King have come to save me!" Grace says with relief, an air of confidence and courage resounding inside of her.

I look at Gwen. She has a demanding look about her, but is trying to cover it up with an imploring tone when she says, "Miles, this poor girl needs our help."

Bors leans close to my ear and whispers, "My King, I'm not so sure we 'ave ta time for t'is. Per'aps on ta return journey…"

But I don't even need time to think about it. I quickly snap, "What kind of king would I be to leave a suffering girl in her time of need? And what kind of knight would you be to leave a damsel in distress?"

Bors straightens up, trying to brush off the insult as gallantly as he can muster. "O' course, my Lord. But I would be amiss 'ad I not advised ye o' the likely consequence o' our actions."

"If you're worried about the Lady of the Lake, don't be. I can help you find her. I know exactly where she is. I'll save you lots of time if you help me!" Grace jumps in excitedly.

I'm shocked. How does she know about our quest?

My bewilderment must be showing on my face because Gwen quickly says, "I told her we can help her. I told her why we are here and that it must be fate that led us to her."

"Yes! It must be God's plan! Too much of a coincidence to just be coincidence. I mean, you're not even on the right path to get to the Enchanted Lake, and I just happened to get into a fight with Father at the exact moment you were coming through the woods, and then the fact that it's—"

"All right, young lass, all right," Bors interrupts Grace's excited explanation, chuckling at her enthusiasm. "Be it fate o' divine providence o' one an' ta same, we are at ye service. But we mustn't waste a moment longer. Ye can explain ye situation on ta way back'ta ta horses."

And with that we begin walking back, Grace chattering happily the whole way. She explains that her father is an old magician, or tries to be, anyway, but is really just a servant to the Lady of the Lake and that the Lady is the real sorceress, the one with real power that just gives her father small tricks to keep him going along as her slave. Her mother, when she was alive, said he hadn't always been so horrid, but the Lady corrupted him over the years with her evil schemes and little tidbits of magic that she shared with him to goad him along. Grace says it got really bad after her mother died, exactly one year ago, because her father is a very lonely man and is now in love with the Lady and will do anything she desires. She explains that she can't run away because despite everything, she still sees the good within her father, and if he is just freed from the will of the Lady of the Lake, she's sure he'll be a righteous person again.

"The Lady is evil, pure evil. She wouldn't even let me give mother a proper burial! Pagan!" Grace says angrily as we approach Ban, Baldwin, and the horses.

"Oh, my! What lovely ponies!" Grace says, running straight for Betsy and petting her lovingly. I guess the girl is easily distracted.

"Ay! What's t'is?" Ban yells, standing up from the feast he and Baldwin apparently created for themselves in our absence.

We walk over to explain the situation and have some

food ourselves. Grace is busy playing with each of the horses and the mule in turn and finally stumbles upon Archimedes in his terrarium strapped to Terry's back.

"Say, what's this? A miniature dragon?"

I laugh. "Yeah, I guess you could say that."

"Amazing!" she yells, and continues to entertain herself with the animals while we discuss our next steps.

"Do you really think the Lady of the Lake is evil? Merlin didn't say anything about her being evil," I ask the group.

"Well, according to legend, no, she isn't really evil. She's an ancient enchantress, been around since time began, so I suppose her values are slightly, perhaps drastically, different from ours. She's seen a lot, lived, if you can call eternal life living, through a lot. She probably just does what she wants to fulfill her desires, even if that means hurting a little girl," Baldwin says.

"Ay. I know ta type," Ban says with a mouthful of venison steak.

"Know a lot o' ancient enchantresses, do ya now?" Bors questions his brother.

Ban drops his food angrily. "Aye. More t'an ye. I met ta Queen o' ta Outer Isles, for one."

"Oh, met her, did ye? An' I 'eard ye snuck around 'er enchanted castle like a whipped pup!"

Ban stands up quickly and his body tenses. "An' 'ow many enchantresses 'ave ye battled, young one?"

Bors stands up slowly, calmly. "Oh, young I am, per'aps. 'Tis why I prefer ta young enchantresses, unlike yeself, who brags 'bout 'is ancient ones!"

"Ya little—" Ban charges his brother and tackles him with full force, better than any tackle I've ever seen. They begin scuffling on the ground, wrestling in the dirt and even striking each other with their fists when they get the chance.

Baldwin, Gwen, and I are powerless to stop them. There's no opening to break them apart. They are like two grizzly bears locked in battle.

"You little brutes, stop acting like children!" comes an incredibly loud yet high-pitched voice. We all turn in astonishment. Even Ban and Bors stop their fighting to see who yelled in such an authoritative manner. Grace is standing, hands on her hips, on top of Phil's saddle. She looks tiny up there on the great stallion, but she sounds like a true leader.

"Stop dilly dallying! Father will start looking for me soon, and if he can't find me, then he'll really be in a rage. We really must be going!"

She jumps down from the giant horse as easily as if she were playing hopscotch and walks over to where Ban and Bors are still locked together and lying on the ground. She grabs each by an ear and pulls them to their feet. They have to stay bent over, though, because she's so short and her arms won't reach their heads if they stand up straight.

"Now, are you two ruffians going to behave yourselves?" Graces asks as sternly as a mother with two misbehaving boys.

"Yes, mum," they both say in synch.

"Good," she releases their ears. "Then let's skedaddle!"

She starts leading the way on foot. The rest of us mount our horses and follow in an orderly fashion.

Chapter Forty

After a few miles of quietly following Grace on horseback, she comes over to us and says, "You'd better tie up your horses here and follow me on foot. Father has hounds that can pick up an unfamiliar scent a mile away. We're downwind now, but better to be safe than sorry!"

"Hounds? Great..." Baldwin says, grabbing a mace from Terry's pile of supplies.

"Oh, you needn't worry. I know all of the commands. It's *Father* who can't take orders. From anyone other than the Lady, of course."

"Well, I'll keep this, just in case," Baldwin says, holding tightly to his weapon.

The rest of us take up our swords, even though we don't plan on using them, and follow Grace on foot. The plan is to reason with her father, explain that he needs to mind his daughter more than any other lady, even if the other lady is an enchantress. And if logic doesn't work, well, I guess we'll just have to play it by ear.

We walk on through some more thick woods, then

C.E. Zyburo

suddenly the trees open up into a rather large clearing in the middle of which sits a ramshackle cottage. It's surprisingly large for being in the middle of nowhere—two stories with a wrap-around porch. It could be a very nice house but it appears destitute now after what can only be years of neglect. Many shingles have blown off the roof and are scattered in the yard close by. Weeds are piling up everywhere and it looks like a decade's worth of leaves haven't been raked. Even the wooden steps leading up to the lop-sided front door are cracked and decaying.

"Some of you guys should spread out around the house. One of the tricks Father learned from the Lady is how to escape. He has all sorts of secret passages and escape routes that even I know nothing about," Grace says.

"All right, you guys form a perimeter. Stand guard at each side of the house. I'll go with Grace," I say.

Gwen looks as if she disagrees with my instructions, but says nothing. She, Ban, Bors, and Baldwin scatter silently to the cardinal directions, taking up their posts.

"All right, young lady, lead the way," I say once everyone's in position.

Grace marches straight up her rotting front steps like a girl on a mission. I'm close behind with Excalibur in my hand, though not raised. I don't want to come across as threatening. Well, not overly threatening, anyway.

"Father, I'm home! And I have something to say!" Grace calls out immediately upon entering the house.

It's dark inside. The only light is that which is being filtered through the dusty windows. The place looks abandoned. Only a few sunken pieces of furniture are scattered about. Some of the massive amounts of leaves from outside have even managed to make their way into the house and have been matted down onto the dirty floorboards making an unintentional, near-permanent mosaic carpet.

"What the heck do you do all day?" I accidentally let slip out of my mouth, referring to the dishevelment of the place.

Grace turns to me with a fierce look in her eyes.

"Are you here to help me or to scold me on my cleaning habits?"

"Oh, sorry," I say abashedly.

"Father!" Grace calls out again, louder than before.

"Eh? What? What do ya want, girl?" comes a harsh-sounding voice from around a corner somewhere.

"He's probably in his study, meddling with some hocus pocus potions. They never work," Grace whispers to me, then yells again, "Father, come out here at once!"

"Don't you dare talk to your father that way!" comes a snarl followed by heavy footsteps lumbering down a hallway. Grace's father appears around the corner and immediately freezes. He's a dirty old man, dirtier even than his daughter, with a scruffy salt-and-pepper beard and scraggy gray hair to his shoulders that appears darkened by soot, as does his face. He's wearing the same type of coarse robe as Grace, but his face isn't nearly as kind. It's not kind at all. It's as harsh as his voice and covered with wrinkles darkened more by anger than by soot.

"What's the meaning of this?" he growls, sounding more like a cornered animal than a man.

"Sir, I mean you no harm. I'm simply here at the

C.E. Zyburo

request of this kind young lady, your daughter," I say as politely and peacefully as possible.

"Bah! Better to have no daughter at all than that creature!"

I'm briefly taken aback by his hatred, but proceed anyway. "Sir, I'm on a quest to find the Lady of the Lake. Your daughter was nice enough to offer my friends and I assistance. She only asked in return that I—"

"*Friends?*" Grace's father interrupts with a hiss before I can finish.

"Yes. I am on a quest with several of my friends. You see, I—"

But the old man is off behind the corner again before I can say another word.

"No use trying to escape, Father! The house is surrounded!" Grace yells after him.

The angry old man comes huffing back in a matter of minutes. He plants himself in the same spot as before, but points an accusatory finger at Grace.

"Curse you, girl! You brought death and destruction to this house! A curse upon you and yours, forever!"

Grace immediately falls to her knees, clasps her hands together, and begins to quietly recite the Lord's Prayer. This must be her defense against her father's curse. I suppose it's not the first time he's cursed her and I gather his curses haven't worked yet.

"Sir, my friends and I are not here to hurt you. We simply wish that you respect your daughter and treat her right."

Grace's father turns his fierce and angry gaze at me, along with his finger, but I continue on.

"You know, my father treats me pretty harshly as you

seem to treat Grace, but I love him all the same, just as I'm sure Grace still loves you. In fact, that's the whole point of my quest—to save my father, and Grace asked us to save you, too. So in a way, both Grace and I are on the same mission, to save our fathers, who we love dearly, and even if they don't often show it, we know they love us as well."

I hold the old man's gaze. Suddenly, he drops his gaze and slowly lowers his finger. He takes a deep breath and sighs. His body seems to become less tense. He seems to relax, in a way. I think my words have struck home. I think he understands what he needs to do, that he's been treating his daughter wrongly for years and needs to make amends. He looks up at me, his eyes appearing much calmer than before.

Without warning the wrath returns. His whole body stiffens with rage and I see that, with his hand closest to the wall he's been disappearing behind, he picks up a long, slender object. It looks like a crowbar.

The old man points his cursing finger at me again and yells, "You'll pay for this transgression!" and charges me, crowbar raised, ready to strike. In an instant he's across the room, only feet away. I don't want to hurt him, so I poise Excalibur over my head for a defensive block. But our iron never meets. For seemingly no reason at all, the old man just collapses in front of me, falling flat on his face, unconscious.

I look up from the old man's body. Grace is standing behind him, a cast iron skillet nearly as big as herself in her hand.

"Grace!" I yell in astonishment.

"What? I didn't kill him. He's just knocked out. I was protecting you!" she says eagerly.

C.E. Zyburo

I roll her father over. He's not bleeding and he's still breathing. Both good signs.

"Well, he's gunna have a heck of a headache when he comes to," I say.

Grace giggles.

"All right, go grab something to tie him up with. We'll just have to take him with us. Can't have him hunting us with his hounds while we go find the Lady of the Lake."

Grace runs off and is back with a good rope in no time. I tie her father's hands and feet—not too tightly though. I still don't aim to hurt the man.

"Be careful. Remember, one of his tricks is escape," Grace warns as I tie the final knot.

"Well, he didn't escape before. And we'll keep our eyes open," I say with a wink.

Grace smiles.

"Okay, let's go," I say, lifting up the old man and tossing his limp body over my shoulder like a sack of potatoes. He's not big but even so he's surprisingly light. Must be Merlin's Magic Energizer, or maybe I'm actually getting stronger.

Chapter Forty-One

"What the heck did you do? You weren't supposed to kill the guy!" Baldwin yells as soon as he sees me carrying Grace's father. The others come trotting over from their locations surrounding the house.

"He's not dead and it wasn't even me who did it! Talk to this little girl!" I say, nodding toward Grace who's standing next to me, a proud grin on her face.

"Father's stubborn. This was the only way!" she explains.

"Well, no use lollygaggin' 'round. Let's go find ta Lady!" Bors says, kindly taking the old man off my shoulders to carry him back to the horses.

The animals are right where we left them but look ready to go. Bors tosses the still unconscious old man onto his horse and jumps up behind him. The rest of us mount our horses in turn.

Ban hoists Grace onto Phil and gets on as well. "Ya can ride wit me, little missuhs. We need ta make up some time," he says.

C.E. Zyburo

"No problem. I love to ride! *Heeya!*" Grace grabs the reins and Phil responds, leading the group of us at a fast pace. But our hustle runs out quickly as the light fades and day turns into night. We are forced to a slow trot and then to a dull trudge as the forest goes completely dark—no stars, no moon, no light is visible except the beams cast by our flashlights guiding the way.

Grace's father wakes up and starts to mumble and mutter foul things as he realizes what's happening, but Bors quickly puts a stop to his angry ramblings with a bandana that he ties around the old man's mouth as a gag. No one objects and soon even the old man himself gives up his struggle and falls asleep.

"How long of a journey?" I call ahead.

"At this rate, we should be there by daybreak," Grace calls back.

Good. Sort of. Only two days to go but it appears we're going to make it.

We plod along ever so slowly, the ground rising up and up as time goes by. We must be at quite a high elevation, but of course there is nothing to see because of the darkness. Somehow, despite our elevation, the woods surrounding us remain as thick as ever. Still, the air is getting thinner and colder, a sure sign that we're climbing ever higher. I can even see my breath now, escaping every time I exhale, forming murky, ominous smoke in the dark that hangs in the air.

The night is silent except for the constant sound of hooves persistently moving forward on the hard ground below. No one has anything to say now that we are getting so close to the end of our journey, the purpose of our quest. We must all be worrying, at least I know I am, if we will be successful, what the Lady of the Lake is like, if she will honor our tokens, and even how we will fulfill the third part of the scroll.

"Cunning of the mind is most important of all,
Outwit the Lady or be doomed to fall."

Funny how I don't even need to look at the Scroll of the Lake any more to remember it word for word. I thought I would need to call on Baldwin to recall the translated text after we had to destroy our phones—and the translation of the scroll on Gwen's phone along with the rest—but it's almost like I can see the exact words of the scroll itself in my mind's eye.

The words of the Scroll of the Lake are burning through my mind all night, so much so that I don't notice the first streaks of sunlight gleaming in the sky as the sun begins to rise.

I only see the growing, but still quite dim light when I hear Grace call back, very quietly, as if she is afraid, "There it is."

All of the horses stop as if by command, although no one had pulled back on their reins. The place has a solemn aura about it that even the horses must be feeling.

It's still too dark to see, but we all know it's there. Some fifty paces ahead, hidden behind the dense fog, is the Lake where the Lady awaits.

"I suppose we should go the rest of the way on foot," I suggest, dismounting Jelly.

"Aye. I don't believe we could get ta 'orses ta move a step furt'er even if we wanted," Ban says, helping Grace down and then getting down himself.

I take Excalibur and everyone else grabs a weapon, though in our minds I'm sure we all realize they'll be useless. Bors successfully takes Grace's father over his shoulder as gently as he can so as not to wake him to avoid more of a fuss. We start moving ahead.

The light is growing steadily though not quickly, but the dense fog ahead doesn't seem to diminish. The only visible sign that there's even a lake ahead is the absence of trees. The mist seems to be covering the lake entirely, and only the lake.

All of us walk up to the shoreline, which is a thin sliver of perfectly round, clear pebbles surrounding the completely still, wave-less water. The mist ends exactly where the water meets the perimeter of beautiful pebbles and rises just high enough so the tallest of us, which is Ban, can't see over the top, even if he tries to peer over by jumping, which he does. It's like the mist is protecting the lake, covering it from view, preventing any outsiders from looking into its secretive waters.

I squint in the direction of what I presume is the middle of the lake, trying to make out anything I can, either in the water or across it. I can't see a thing, but suddenly it looks as if the mist is moving, slowly moving in wisps, slowly moving toward the group of us on the shore.

I start to tell everyone what I see, but they've all noticed the same thing.

"She's coming," Grace whispers.

We all stand as still as statues as the wisps of mist move ever closer. Once they are about twenty feet away, the fog either clears enough for me to tell what's coming, or the fog itself turns into the figure. I'm not really sure which, but before I know it, an exotic, gorgeous woman is approaching me, walking gracefully yet purposefully, on the surface of the water. She's like no woman I've ever seen before. I don't even feel comfortable calling her a woman, for she's so different from every other woman it doesn't seem right to use this word to describe her. She's tall and slender and moves with the fluidity of water. She's dressed in a delicate, flowing gown of the purest blue imaginable that's reflected upon her softly toned skin, or perhaps it's her complexion which is of an other-worldly color that's being reflected by her gown—it's impossible to say. Her translucent hair flows the length of her train, extending far behind her bare feet, but it doesn't drag, it seems to float behind her. Everything about her seems to float and flow. She is, most assuredly, the one I have been seeking—the Lady of the Lake.

She walks straight up to me and stops only inches from my face. Her eyes are like the pebbles beneath my feet—beautiful and nearly transparent, like perfectly polished spheres of quartz. She seems to study me with those magic eyes, then, in the most hypnotizing voice imaginable, says,

"I see the Great King has returned."

I open my mouth to say—I don't know what—and nothing comes out. It really is as if I'm being hypnotized by her presence alone.

"Don't fall for her sorcery! She's a witch!" Grace screams, and as before with her father, falls to her knees and begins praying.

The Lady turns calmly toward Grace.

"Oh, you brought the precious child. And her father too, I see."

She looks at the old man on Bors' shoulder.

"Better he stays asleep so as not to disturb us."

C.E. Zyburo

The Lady raises her hand in the old man's direction. She says nothing and nothing seems to happen, but I assume she cast a sleeping spell on the old man without even uttering a word.

Everyone remains silent. We all just stare at the ravishing Lady. Only Grace's soft whispering of prayer can be heard. The rest of the world seems to have stopped entirely.

The Lady turns back to me.

"So, Young Arthur, I presume you have come to claim the King's Scabbard."

I manage to find my voice, though my words come out awkwardly and seem not to be entirely mine. "Ye... Yes, my Lady. I have brought the tokens that the Scroll of the Lake demanded."

I turn to grab the armor of the three defeated dark knights from Terry's back, only to realize that the horses were left behind in the wood.

The Lady of the Lake laughs, a quiet, soft, laugh like the flutter of a bird's wings.

"Yes, I'm sure the armor is splendid. And what of the second token?"

"Yes, my Lady," I say, and without thinking, without any seeming control over my own actions, I remove my shirt to show the Lady my scars.

She reaches out her hand to feel my nearly-healed wounds. Her touch is so light I can hardly feel it. It's like water trickling softly over my skin.

"You are courageous indeed, Young Arthur."

Gwen scoffs. The Lady turns to look at her, seemingly only noticing her presence now that she made a sound.

"Oh, pardon me," Gwen says. "Yes, he is very courageous. So, are you happy with the tokens? If so, we'll be happy to trade for the scabbard and be on our way."

The Lady smiles.

"Perhaps the future King would do best to make such a decision."

She turns to me. I haven't been able to take my gaze from her. It's as if I'm in a trance.

"Young Arthur, would you like the scabbard?"

"Yes, my Lady," I respond robotically.

"Then come with me."

The Lady turns as if she's about to walk back into the fog over the lake. I start to follow her without a thought, without a care.

"Miles!" Gwen grabs my arm and holds me next to her. "What about Grace? What about her father?"

Only with Gwen's touch am I able to pull my gaze away from the Lady of the Lake. As I turn to face Gwen, out of the corner of my eye the Lady seems to freeze, but only for a second. Her ever-present fluidity seems to go rigid for a moment, but she returns to her usual state as she turns back to Gwen and I.

I'm looking at Gwen now, though, at those golden, heavenly eyes I fell in love with the first time I saw them. I know I love her and only her, forever. She'll always be there to support me, to save me. She'll be my queen forever and I'll love her always.

I brush back her soft hair behind her ear, even though I don't need to. She looks perfect no matter what. I just have an unquenchable desire to touch her, to feel her, to be near her.

I smile, and say comfortingly, "I won't forget Grace or her father. I'll make sure they're both accounted for, that they're both provided for." I lean close to Gwen and press my forehead against hers, closing my eyes as I say softly, "And I'll never forget about you. I love you. I'll always love you."

I tilt my head to kiss Gwen. Our lips meet. I feel a sensation I never have before—pure and utter joy. Ecstasy. It's more than fireworks. It's paradise. It's heaven.

I pull away and brush her hair back once again, just because. She's holding back tears. She's beautiful.

"I'll be back soon," I say.

Gwen's lips are trembling, but she's strong.

The Lady of the Lake turns and starts walking into the fog, into the center of the lake.

I start to follow, taking my first steps onto the lake. The water doesn't part, I don't form a single ripple with my feet. I'm walking on water.

I take a few more steps and my hand begins to separate from Gwen's. Our hands had apparently intertwined during our kiss. I hadn't even noticed.

"I love you," I say as our fingers move apart and our final touch is broken.

"I love you too," Gwen replies.

She is all the protection I'll ever need. Her love is my shield against any lady's enchantment. There's no room in my heart for anyone else but Gwen.

I step into the mist, confident in my ability to deter any enchantment the Lady of the Lake may attempt.

Chapter Forty-Two

The Lady of the Lake must know the power of Gwen's and my love, because she doesn't try any more of her funny hypnotizing business. As we walk out ever farther into the center of the lake, walking through the mist, walking *on* water, she begins to speak quite bluntly, not in the dreamy, mesmerizing tone she'd used before.

"So, Young Arthur, I see you've already found your soul mate. Good for you. Unfortunately, though, I would have made a much mightier, a much more feared, a much more treacherous queen. But..." she flicks her wrist as if to say it's no big deal, perhaps it was even expected, "...it's not in our destiny, as they say, for us to rule together."

I have my full wits about me now and I have no trouble finding the right words. Well, maybe not the *right* words, but the words I myself am thinking and wish to speak, anyway. So I blurt out, "You mean you wanted to marry me?"

The Lady of the Lake laughs heartily. Not like her

subtle laugh before, but a full laugh. A laugh that even has a little air of evil to it.

"You are a silly boy. It's not *you* I wanted to marry, it was your throne. I simply want to be queen! But alas! I suppose I shall have to wait another millennia for my next chance. Oh well. What's another thousand years for a Lady Eternal," she says with a sigh. "So, how did you find the tasks of the quest? You obviously fulfilled the first two with great success, but were they difficult? Did you find gallantry and chivalry everything you expected?"

"Well, my Lady, I'm quite glad I only had to do battle with conjured knights. I just wouldn't feel right taking another person's life, no matter who he is."

"Hmm… Interesting… Time does change people, it would seem. You used to be such a warrior."

"I still am. But why fight an enemy I have no real issue with? I have no issue with my half-sister. I've never even met the girl!"

The Lady turns to me with a confused look, the first look of confusion I've seen on her face. It doesn't suit her. But she isn't confused herself; she appears to think I'm confused.

"Your half-sister? Morgan LeFay? Is that who you think you've been battling on your quest?"

The Lady's raised eyebrows straighten along with her lips. She laughs again, but this time is clearly laughing at me.

"My dear boy, the knights you have been facing were sent by me! Even the dragon was mine! A dear pet, that, I must say, I am quite disappointed to have lost. Oh well. I have others."

Now I'm really confused.

"You? You're the enemy who's been sending these things to attack me?" I grip Excalibur tightly in my hand, expecting anything now.

The Lady continues walking, speaking kindly to me over her shoulder. She acts and speaks at ease, but I'm still on edge, still on guard, even though I have no choice but to follow her.

"Enemy? No. I'm not your enemy. But you can't expect me to simply hand over the King's Scabbard to just anyone, now do you? No, you had to prove yourself. You had to complete the tasks of the Scroll of the Lake. I didn't write them for nothing."

Things are starting to make a little more sense now, but, as always, I still have more questions than answers.

"But Merlin said my half-sister was the one I had to watch out for."

"Oh, Merlin is an old fool! His lore is almost as bad as his magic. Certainly, you will have to deal with Morgan LeFay. She will be more of a danger to you than I, but not on this quest. On this quest you had to deal with me. And you have done exceedingly well."

"But what about the third task? What about outwitting you?"

If she wrote the Scroll of the Lake, and she knows I am supposed to outwit her, then how the heck am I going to do so? This must be some kind of trick, or worse, some kind of trap…

"Oh, that silly task? It's nothing. I like you, Arthur. I always have. You can have the King's Scabbard. It is there."

She stops and directly below where I'm standing, through crystal clear water, laying at the bottom of the lake, I see the King's Scabbard. Its ancient beauty of the most skillfully crafted leather and gold shimmers up through the depths of the pristine water.

"Just like that? You're just going to give it to me?" I ask in disbelief.

The Lady of the Lake shrugs her shoulders as if it doesn't matter.

"If that is all you desire of me, then yes."

I have a mind to take her offer. I don't have any more time to waste. My *father* doesn't have any more time to waste. In a day, he'll be dead unless I can get this scabbard into his hand...

But the scabbard isn't all I need from the Lady—and she knows it. I made a promise, a king's oath, to save a little girl, and I'm not about to break it.

"And what do you need as payment to release Grace's father from your servitude?" I ask bluntly.

But the Lady is still acting coy. If she can't hypnotize me and enchant me with spells, apparently playing dumb is her game.

"Hmm? Oh, *him*. You don't want *him*. He's a dreadful fellow, a bore really. He shall remain mine. You wouldn't want him and I wouldn't want to burden you with him. And you...well, you can have the girl. Do what you will with her. Another gift from the ever generous, always gracious, Lady of the Lake."

Yeah, right. And humble, too.

"I can't do that," I say. "She needs her father. She believes he's a good man. Answer me straight—what must I do to get you to release him?"

The Lady's eyes flash, but she quickly recovers and hides her wrath behind soft tones.

"Oh, I see. Directly to the point. Such are the times; such are the ways of men. Very well. In exchange for the old man's life, you must make me your queen."

I shudder at the mere thought of it. Her, the Lady of the Lake, my queen? It is not that she seems so evil, as Grace believes, and she is far from unpleasing to the eye, she just seems…terrible. In form and power, she terrifies me, like a wild animal merely posing as one that's tame.

The Lady must see the doubt brewing inside me. She quickly adds, "Oh, I know you love that *other* girl. I do not mean to take you away from her, of course. Fate would never allow it. You may see her as often as you wish." The Lady comes next to me. "And I will never say a word. And I will never bother you." She comes closer, touching my arm, and whispers in my ear, "Unless you should desire me." She steps back and resumes her normal composure. "Discretion is one of my many charms, and as I've said already, it is not *you* I want, it is your throne."

Can she really mean all this? And what would Gwen say? Surely Gwen would never approve of such a deal, even to save Grace's father. Or would she?

"Oh, and there is one more thing. A great benefit to you, in fact. Should you choose me as your queen, you will avoid the awful death at the hand of your own son that Merlin has no doubt foretold. So you see, your dearly beloved should really be thanking me for making you such an offer. It will spare you an atrocious death and will save her from much heartbreak and grief."

"How do you know that?" I ask, not sure if I can trust her.

She gestures above her head, moving wisps of mist in the process.

"It is written in the stars."

She looks at me, waiting for an answer.

What can I do? What *should* I do? Maybe Gwen would be okay with the situation, knowing I only love her, knowing my marriage to the Lady of the Lake will only be for show...

"No," I say out loud, still thinking to myself, but I already know the answer. I know the right choice in my heart, in my soul, that's crying out in response. "No, I cannot honor that request."

The Lady's eyes look as if they are on fire. Her flowing figure becomes rigid once again. For a brief instant, she no longer appears to be the Lady of the Lake at all, but more like the Lady of the Sun. She's bright—glaring—with rage. But only for a moment. Again, she somehow composes herself quickly and acts as if nothing happened, as if my response didn't bother her in the least and she hasn't a care in the world.

"So be it. Well, then, since you are so keen on keeping promises, just promise to grant me one wish in the future, just one, as a token of good faith. For, you see, there is nothing you have that I desire. The scabbard and the old man are mine, my Lord, but if you will give me a gift when I ask it, you shall have both."

I think about this new offer. It's definitely better than the first. Perhaps I'm fulfilling the last task of the Scroll of the Lake. Or maybe the Lady of the Lake is still playing me for the fool. Is this another one of her tricks or am I *"outwitting the Lady"* after all? There's no way to be sure. Still, my time, my father's time, is running out, and I doubt if the Lady will make me many more offers. I have to take this deal.

"So long as you do not ask to be my queen, I will make this promise. One gift. You shall have *one* gift of your choosing in exchange for the scabbard and the freedom of Grace's father. On my honor, I will give you anything you ask for."

"Done."

The Lady of the Lake smiles, a smile that looks more like a concealed sneer. But I can't worry about that now. I have to save my dad.

"I'll take the scabbard now," I say, wanting to go on my way and find my dad as soon as possible.

"It is yours. Take it. I will ask for my gift when the time comes."

And with that and a swirl into the mist, the Lady of the Lake is gone. Just as she disappears, so does the solid earth on which I stand. SPLASH! I'd forgotten I'm walking on water. Now I'm in the lake, trying to stay afloat in my heavy clothes while keeping Excalibur in my hand. Apparently the Lady only needed me to walk with her for conversation until our negotiations had ended and a deal was struck. Now I'm on my own.

I flounder for a moment until I'm able to keep my head comfortably above the frigid mountain water. No use wasting time and risking hypothermia. I take a deep breath and dive straight down, using Excalibur as best as I can manage as a type of underwater oar. The scabbard's still at the bottom of the lake, and it's much deeper than I'd expected. Because the water's so clear, it had looked to be closer than it really is. Luckily, part of Dad's warrior training included aquatics. A large part, actually. He was a Navy Seal, after all. Had it not been for his grueling regimen, I probably would never have been able to

218

retrieve the scabbard, but, despite it being so far down that the water pressure makes my ears feel like they're going to explode, I reach the scabbard on my first attempt.

I push off the rocky bottom and make it to the surface just as my breath gives out. Now for the long swim to shore.

Chapter Forty-Three

Ban is the first to see me through the ever-present thick fog, struggling to make it back from the middle of the lake. He immediately jumps in the water, not even pausing to remove his boots. He helps me swim ashore and we both lie panting on the grass, not wanting to touch the freezing water even with our feet.

Gwen comes running over to us.

"Bors! Baldwin! Give them your clothes! Ban, Miles, take off those wet rags or you'll freeze to death!"

Ban starts stripping down, but I'm still too exhausted to move. Gwen assists in changing me.

"Let's get back to the horses and make a fire," Gwen says.

Baldwin comes over and helps me to my feet. "You were gone a long time, my King. We were getting worried. You didn't—I mean—did you…" He seems to be struggling to find the right words.

I'm still trying to recuperate and can only stumble along with Baldwin's support, but I manage to stammer, teeth chattering, "Out with it."

"Well, I see you got the scabbard. Did you happen to make a promise in exchange?"

I'm surprised Baldwin could know that. I nod, more than a bit concerned.

Baldwin lowers his gaze and nods in response, "Well, you did what had to be done. We'll just worry about it later."

We all walk over to where Grace is staring at us. She has fear in her eyes.

"Did, did you save my father?" she asks worriedly.

I ruffle her hair.

"Yes, little one. The Lady released him from her service."

Grace immediately embraces me as tears of joy start flowing forth.

"Oh, thank you, thank you, King Arthur. Thank you."

I get such a feeling of happiness for the girl that there are no words I can say to her. There's a lump in my throat, anyway, so I just enjoy our hug and say nothing.

"Say, where tid tat ol' man get ta, anyhow?" Bors asks, looking around.

We all do the same, but we don't see Grace's father anywhere. He's nowhere to be found. He must have slipped out of his restraints and...

The supplies! Our horses! Archimedes!

Thinking Grace's father ran off with our belongings is the first thing that goes through my mind and, judging by the look on everyone else's face, they are worrying about the same thing.

Without warning, there's a mad rustling noise from back in the brush. It sounds like horses on the move. We all raise our weapons, which we luckily had on us when the rest of our supplies were taken, ready for whatever foe is about to spring at us from behind the trees.

But instead of a group of enemies charging us, out of the forest come all of our horses, and the mule, in their orderly line, being led by none other than Grace's father. He's beaming with joy and humming a happy tune. He looks ten years younger than when I first saw him. All of the hatred that's drained from his body must have taken away some years with it.

Grace's father leads the horses, and Terry, straight to the shore of the lake.

"Drink up, my boys! Oh, and girl, of course. Beggin' your pardon, miss."

He makes a kindly bow to Betsy. All of the animals lower their heads and begin taking hearty gulps of the refreshing, pure mountain lake water.

"Father? Is it really you? Are you...okay?" Grace asks, taking slow, tentative steps toward the obviously changed man.

He smiles and squats down to be eye level with his daughter. Tears start forming in his eyes.

"Oh, Gracey. Yes, it's me. It's your father. I'm back, little baby. I'm back for good and I'll never go away again."

He opens his arms to her. Grace runs to him and buries herself in his chest. Both father and daughter begin to sob, so happy they are together as they were meant to be. Even I start to tear up again, but manage to hold it back.

"Now 'ow tid ya get ta horses down 'ere, might I ask? T'ey were stiff as boards when we left 'em!" Ban asks, patting Phil's side happily.

"Oh, they just needed a good talkin' to, is all. This water is the best, most rejuvenating water you'll find anywhere. They need it for their return journey, as do you. Drink up!"

And we do. And the water is delicious. The most wholesome, crisp water I've ever had.

After our brief reprieve, Grace's father turns to me and says, "Now, I would treat you to a fine meal back at my home, but I suppose you've got to make haste. Saving *your* father, was it? There's no gratitude I can express for saving my daughter's, but if there is anything I can do, ever, just name it and it will be done."

He grabs my hand and shakes it, sealing the bond with his word.

"Thank you," I say, "Yes, I really do need to get going as quickly as possible. I only have a day left..." I scratch my head in dismay. "How on earth can I get to my dad in a day? I don't even know where he is...and I'm in the middle of the woods with only a horse for transportation!" I say more to myself than to anyone else.

But Grace's father hears me and smiles.

"Oh, come on now, young man. Where there's a will, there's a way. I believe I spotted something that may help you..."

He walks over to where Terry is now relaxing and munching on some nice, green grass after having his fill of water, and pulls out a little vial from one of the packs on his back. He even takes out Archimedes from his terrarium and brings him over.

"Now, I may not be a good magician, but I do believe I know what these two things, in combination, may be good for. The Lady of the Lake has her own pets, remember," he says, handing me the vial and Archimedes.

I look around at all of my companions. Archimedes will only grow large enough to carry two or three of us at most, and if I want to make the fastest time possible, which I do, the lighter the load the better.

"Don't you worry about your friends, now," Grace's father says, reading the thoughts behind my worried face. "They can stay with Grace and I as long as they desire. We have plenty of room and haven't been making good use of it over the past few years. They'll get well rested and I'll load them up with plenty of supplies for their return journey. I make the best turkey jerky this side of the Mississippi! Haha!"

I look around at my friends' faces once more. They all nod in approval. Ban comes up and slaps me, hard, on the back.

"Good luck ta ye, my King. We shall see one anot'er again, soon."

Bors walks up next and gives me a great big bear hug that squeezes the very air out of my lungs.

"I'll save some o' ta jerky for ya," he says.

Grace runs over and hugs me, only slightly less tightly than Bors.

"Thank you, thank you, thank you. You are a great king. And the best knight ever!"

She runs back to her dad and holds his hand.

Then Baldwin steps up awkwardly and shakes my hand, saying, "See ya back at Caerleon."

What a goofy guy.

And finally it's Gwen's turn. She puts her hand on my cheek, caressing me lovingly, her golden eyes somehow showing joy and concern at the same time.

"I'm so proud of you," she says, stroking my hair. "I know you'll save your father. Don't worry about us. Just finish this thing and we'll all be together again. I love you."

"I love you, too," I say. I lean over and kiss Gwen, my love, my angel. I feel the same as before, I feel I'm in heaven. I doubt if that feeling will ever go away. Gwen is my everything.

She steps back with the others.

I put Archimedes on the ground and hold the vial above him. I take out the stopper and delicately pour one drop of the enchanted concoction onto his back.

"*Dominus opem ferat illi alae!*" I say.

Immediately his wings sprout and he starts to grow. In a matter of moments he is fully dragon-size and ready to fly.

I attach the King's Scabbard to my belt, sheath Excalibur, and jump on Archimedes' back.

"Don't forget some food!" Grace yells and tosses up a satchel full of supplies.

"Thanks," I say. "See you all soon. Let's go, Archimedes!"

And just like that we're off, soaring through the air, my friends disappearing under the canopy of trees in an instant.

"Stay in the clouds so no one sees us. Wouldn't want to be shot down by fighter jets or anything," I say, and Archimedes listens. I always knew he was smart.

It feels great up here and it's easy to stay on his back. His scales hold me well and I can hold onto the prickly spines at the back of his head for extra support. Not that I need it, really, since he's the size of a bus, but it's still a little nerve-wracking being hundreds if not thousands of feet in the air with no seatbelt or fuselage surrounding me.

The problem now is that I don't know where to find Dad. I suppose the only way is to find out where the president is. My dad's last message said he'd be on detail with the president, so wherever he is, that's where Dad will be. And the best way to find the president? The news, of course.

"Archimedes, get close to the bottom of the cloud line and be on the lookout for an isolated gas station or something."

He complies and in a matter of minutes we spot what looks like a gas station or convenience store pretty much in the middle of nowhere. It's on a small country road and has only one car parked in front.

"There! Land in the back as quietly as you can," I say.

There are no trees around to hide in, so the back of the building is our best option and I don't have any time to waste looking for a better spot.

Archimedes starts a slow, circular descent and in a few seconds, we're on the ground behind the small building.

Chapter Forty-Four

"Stay here. Any sign of trouble, just make some noise and I'll come out quick," I tell Archimedes.

He lowers his body flat to the ground and closes his wings. He actually blends in fairly well with the dirt and luckily the only windows at the back of the building are tiny and high up on the wall so Archimedes is out of view. We may just get out of this yet.

I walk around to the front of the building and quickly realize it's not a gas station or convenience store at all. It's a bar. The bright red neon sign in the front window that says "BAR" kind of gives it away.

"Well, I'll just have to pretend to be old," I tell myself, and strut through the front door as if nothing were awry.

The bar is really dark and smells of stale smoke, exactly what I'd expect for such a random establishment. It's a small place—a couple of booths along the back wall, the bar on the left with only four stools, and that's it. I wonder where people go to the bathroom.

227

I pull out a stool and sit down, leaning my elbows on the bar. It's sticky. I pull back and keep my hands in my lap. There appears to be a little room behind the bar with fluorescent lighting. That must be where the owner of the one car in the lot, the bartender I surmise, must be because I'm alone in the small, dingy bar area. But I'm not leaving because there's a small TV in the corner attached to the wall next to the ceiling and I need to see the news.

I cough loudly, trying to get someone's attention. A head peers out from the lighted room. A body follows.

"Sorry, didn't hear ya come in," the lady says while chewing gum. She's quite pretty and dressed in all black, matching the atmosphere with her outfit but not her looks.

I put on my most adult face and voice and say, "No problem. Mind turning on the news?"

She looks at me kind of funny. I hope she doesn't notice I'm underage and kick me out. It might just be dark enough in here that she doesn't see how young I am.

She turns and stretches as high as she can to turn on the TV.

"Remote doesn't work," she says as the screen begins to brighten. "Sure ya want the news? Most guys want sports."

"Nah. The news please. It's kind of important."

"All right, suit yourself," she changes the channel until she finds what I want and stops. "Ugh, so boring. You better tip me well for this," she turns around and leans over the bar directly in front of me, rather seductively in such a low-cut shirt, I must say. "So, what can I get ya?"

"Uh...beer please," I say, trying to avoid staring down.

228

She laughs and blows a bubble with her gum. "Beer, huh? What kind of beer?"

Uh oh. Am I caught?

"Umm…whatever you recommend," I say.

She reaches below the bar and pulls out a bottle dripping with cold condensation and little bits of ice. She cracks it open, at the same time popping a bubble with her teeth, and slides the beer to me.

She chuckles again. "Here's my recommendation for such a slick kid."

I hold the cold beer in my hand and say nothing. Kid? Did she just call me a kid? I just pretend like it makes no difference to me and stare at the TV. She's still leaning over and staring at me, but I ignore her. The news is about to start talking politics.

"So, where ya from?" she asks.

I guess I should be polite and keep up the conversation so I don't get kicked out. Besides, I can read the captions on the TV so I don't really need to hear what they're saying, anyway.

"Virginia," I say, not wanting to get too specific.

The bartender chews her gum loudly.

"VA, huh? You're a long way from home."

The newscaster is saying the President's trip is reportedly going well. But trip to where?

"Yeah, just on vacation," I say, still reading the captions.

"Vacation? Why the heck are ya vacationing in Bloomfield, Wyoming?"

So that's where I am. Okay, that helps a little. Now if I can only find out where the president is…

"Uh…just a road trip," I say, not really paying

attention to the conversation now because I think the anchorman is about to say where the president is giving his next speech...

"Oh, a road trip. Sounds nice. Wish I could go on one of those. Hey, I didn't get your name. I'm Liz Avalon."

"Miles Arthur," I say mechanically.

There it is! The text reads:

"The President is at the summit in Mexico City for one more day...and in other news, three missing children from..."

"I gotta go!" I say, excitedly jumping from my barstool and heading for the door.

"Hey! Ya didn't pay for that beer!" the bartender says, ducking under an open area of the bar to follow me.

"Oh, uh, sorry!" I yell over my shoulder, not daring to pause. "I'll send you the money. Liz Everton of Bloomfield, Wyoming!"

I'm running out the door and around the building, but the bartender's in hot pursuit and still on my tail.

"Liz *Avalon*, and that's not how this works!" she yells after me.

But she's too late. I've reached the back of the building. Archimedes perks up as soon as he sees me hauling around the corner. I hop onto his back in one swift jump and call out, "Fly quick, Archimedes! Head south! We're going to Mexico!"

Archimedes begins to take off just as Liz rounds the corner. She stops in her tracks when she catches sight of Archimedes.

"Holy—!"

I can't hear her over the thunderous beat of

C.E. Zyburo

Archimedes' great wings, and I'm not sure if she can hear me, but I yell down anyway, "Sorry, Liz! I'll send you the money! I promise!"

And just like that Archimedes and I are back in the clouds and heading south for Mexico City.

Chapter Forty-Five

The landscape changes dramatically as Archimedes flies through the air as fast as he can manage. We fly all day and we stay in the clouds most of the time, of course, but occasionally drop below them to view the landscape, which is, right now, our only way of knowing how far south we've travelled. The rocky, mountainous outcroppings of Wyoming and Colorado are quickly replaced by the flat plains of New Mexico and/or Texas. I'm not quite sure which state we're over, but based on my rudimentary knowledge of U.S. geography, it's got to be one of those two.

Upon our next check, the plains have given way to dry, arid, southwestern-style flatlands. Not quite desert, but not far from it, either. We must be getting close to the border.

"Stay low, Archimedes," I tell him. "Just below the cloud line."

We've been travelling for several hours now, so we must be getting close. And then I see it, the landmark I've been waiting for.

C.E. Zyburo

"The Rio Grande!" I yell as we fly over the vast river. "We're getting close now!"

But as I look at the beautiful sight, an airplane comes into view, close enough to startle both Archimedes and I with the sounds of its engines.

"Get back in the clouds!" I scream. And we do, but not before I realize we were close enough to be spotted by the pilots or passengers.

"I hope they didn't see us. We should probably land, just in case. Find a town with some forests close by, Archimedes. I need to stop in a store and get a map, anyway."

We quickly spot an adequate area and Archimedes lands in some thick woods close by.

"I'll be back soon," I say, and walk toward the town.

I still have no money, but I really need a map or I'll never find Mexico City. I guess I'll have to steal it. Borrow it, really. I'll send the money to the store just like I'm going to send money to Liz Avalon of Bloomfield, Wyoming.

I walk into the first convenience store I see, one that looks like any you'd find on any street corner in America. There are a few other customers, so maybe it will be easy to steal a map. I hope it will be, anyway, but first, I need to find out where I am to get my bearings straight.

I walk up to the guy behind the cash register. He's a tall, thin Mexican man with a dark moustache.

"Dónde estoy?" I say in my best attempt at a Spanish accent. "Qué es la llame de esta ciudad?"

Boy, I sure hope my one-and-a-half years of Spanish will work.

The guy stares at me with an odd look on his face,

233

then bursts out laughing. He finally calms down and says, "My man, you are close to the border. We all speak English here. The place is called Ojinaga."

"Oh," I say, rather embarrassed. "Estoy embarazado."

The man looks at me and falls into hysterics again.

"Give the Spanish a rest, hombre," he says, wiping the tears from his cheeks. "You just said you are pregnant!"

Yikes.

"Okay, thanks. Do you have any maps of Mexico?" I ask.

"Of course! In the back, there," he says, pointing.

"Thanks," I say again, scared to even say "gracias" should I be wrong about that, too.

I walk to the map stand in the back. When I get to the maps I find the one I need. On one side it is topographical and on the other political, so it will be easy to find Mexico City. Just need to travel southeast, which will be easy to tell with the sun. Now, to steal the map...

The cashier is busy with some other customers, so I quickly make my move, shoving the map under my belt and shirt. I start to walk out of the store.

"Don't need that map anymore, my man?" the cashier asks as I push open the door.

"Uh, no. I know where I am now. Thanks," I say, concealing my nervousness as best as I can.

"All right. Ciao," he says, going back to his work.

"Hasta luego," I say, stepping out of the door.

Once I'm a few paces away from the storefront, I sprint to the trees where Archimedes is hiding. I lean on him, panting.

"Phew! That was close! I need a drink!" I say, and for

the first time I open the satchel Grace had tossed me. Inside is a flask of water, plenty of dried venison, and luckily, a flask of Merlin's Magic Energizer.

"Awesome!" I exclaim, about to take a hefty swig. But before I do I look at Archimedes, who is basically whimpering like a begging puppy.

"Oh, sorry! And you're the one doing all the work! Here, have a drink of this," I say, tilting the flask of Merlin's potion so Archimedes can have a sip. "It burns, but it works wonders."

Archimedes ends up drinking the whole thing and even swallows all of the venison in one gulp. He deserves the modest feast, though, and definitely needs it for the rest of the journey more than I do.

"All right, let's go. Head southeast and stay in the clouds," I say once we're done fueling up. Archimedes takes off like a rocket. That magic concoction certainly does the trick!

At this pace, I estimate we'll make it to Mexico City in about ten hours. It will be cutting it close, but it *should* give me just enough time to find and save Dad.

It starts to get dark almost as soon as we begin the second leg of our international flight. Day becomes night abruptly.

I must fall asleep immediately because the next thing I know I'm waking up to the beautiful colors of the sunrise overhead. But it doesn't feel like I'm moving. I sit up and realize I'm not. I'm still on Archimedes' back, but he's lying on the ground, not flying.

"Archimedes! What are you doing? We have to get to Mexico City!" I yell, jumping to the ground.

But he continues to lie where he is. He just looks at

me and tilts his head to one side, then looks to the right. I follow his gaze. Nothing but trees.

"What? What is it?" I ask. He continues staring, so I walk in the direction he is looking.

I walk a few paces through the trees and then suddenly in the distance I see it—a giant urban metropolis full of streets and buildings, but not yet many people because it is so early in the morning. Mexico City!

I run back to Archimedes.

"Thank you! I didn't realize! You did great! Thank you, buddy!"

I rub his chest and scratch behind his ears. He immediately begins to shrink and in a minute he's back to normal bearded dragon size and his wings are gone.

I hook Excalibur in its scabbard to my belt, throw my satchel over one shoulder, and place Archimedes on the other.

"Let's go find Dad," I say, and start marching into the great, sprawling city.

C.E. Zyburo

Chapter Forty-Six

Mexico City is a vast, rambling municipality made up of hundreds and thousands of concrete buildings. But the main streets, for the most part, are lined up in a grid pattern, so my going is not all that slow or tedious. Still, it would be nice if I could hop on a bus or catch a cab, but without money, that's not going to happen.

More and more people begin to crowd the streets as the morning sun climbs higher into the sky. The dull city silence of the dawn is quickly replaced with the typical buzzing of any modern city—cars starting and driving off, doors opening and closing, the heavy sound of a million footsteps on the pavement headed to any number of dreary city jobs. But the weather's nice, much warmer than Wyoming, and so seem the people. I'm actually feeling fairly optimistic about getting this thing done on time.

I check my watch. It's 10:25 a.m. Less than four hours to go. I really should make sure I'm headed in the right direction. So far I've been walking away from the mountainous, woodsy outskirts that surround the city and heading straight for the center of town where all of the skyscrapers are clustered together. I'm assuming somewhere downtown is where the president, and therefore my dad, will be, but I've got to be sure. I've got to ask someone.

I stop the friendliest-looking man on the street, one in a button-down but not a suit. A businessman probably wouldn't stop to help a kid, especially one carrying a sword and a bearded dragon on his shoulder, but so far no one's bothered me and this guy looks like he'll help.

"Señor, dónde ..." oh wait, I forgot—he probably speaks English. I start over. "Do you speak English?"

"Yes," he says in a lovely accent. He checks out my getup and looks at Archimedes but doesn't run away. That's a good start.

"Do you know where the president is? Of the United States? He's supposed to be at a summit here today."

"Oh, of course. Everyone knows about the Peace Summit. It's being held at the Palacio Nacional."

I guess the man assumes I know where that is, but I don't.

"Where's that?"

"It's at El Zócalo, of course."

I'm still lost.

"La Plaza de la Constitución? The main square?"

No idea.

The man grabs my bearded dragon-free shoulder and points straight down the street we're standing on.

"Oye. Take this street, Avenida Instituto Politécnico Nacional, all the way to a big intersection of highways. Once you pass that, take a left on any of the streets until

you see Eje Central Lázaro Cárdenas and take a right.
You want to head south. El Zócalo is south from here.
You have to go a long way and you'll pass La Plaza de las
Tres Culturas, pero that's not it. You keep going south,
always south, until you hit Avenida Cinco de Mayo and
take a left. The Palace of Fine Arts is right there so you
can't miss it. Just follow Cinco de Mayo and you'll find
El Zócalo. Okay?"

The man starts walking away. I got some of that, but
by no means the whole thing.

"Wait!" I call after the man who is now walking in
the opposite direction I need to go. "How long do you
think it will take?"

"On foot?" he calls back over his shoulder. "Hours,
mi amigo, hours. This is Mexico City!" and he's gone.

Well, I guess I better get started. I walk straight down
the street I'm on, whatever it's called. The street sign says
Avenida Instituto Politécnico Nacional. Not very catchy.
Okay, what was the next street after that? Some big
intersection, but the directions after that I already forgot!
Great...

But the man did say I'm looking for the Palacio
Nacional. Even my limited Spanish tells me that means
National Palace. And he kept saying an unfamiliar word a
bunch of times. What was it... Zócalo? Yeah, that was it!
El Zócalo! So that must be important, too.

I try to remember all of the directions, to no avail, but
I know I'm looking for the National Palace and the
Zócalo, whatever that is, so maybe that will be enough.

After what seems like an hour of walking, I approach
the major intersection the man described. He was
right—you can't miss it. It looks like ten highways are all

crisscrossing over and under each other. It's like a messy pile of concrete spaghetti.

It takes me another ten minutes of walking, but I get through it. It's now almost 11a.m. and I'm lost again.

What did the guy say to do next?

I have no idea.

Guess I'll have to ask someone else.

I approach a nicely-dressed woman and ask, "Do you know where—"

But she brushes past me without even a glance in my direction before I can even finish my question.

Not very polite.

I realize this must happen to homeless people every day, and I vow never to ignore someone like that, someone in need, ever again, but I have no time to brood over it. On to the next person.

I decide to make my question short and sweet to try and avoid being ignored. As the next person walks near me, I simply ask, "El Zócalo?"

It works! The lady doesn't stop walking, she doesn't even pause, but she does point down a street to the left.

I'm hot on the trail, now!

I make great progress like this, walking on and on through the seemingly endless city streets, pausing only to ask "El Zócalo?" when I feel like I need to make a turn. I only get turned around once and, like the first guy who gave me directions said, the Zócalo is almost always to the south.

But finally I make it, unmistakably, to the mysterious location I've been seeking— El Zócalo.

It's a giant plaza—huge—surrounded on all sides by beautiful, old stone buildings, two of which stand out more than the others. To the north stands a great, majestic building with two towers soaring high above everything else in the plaza. It must be a cathedral. The other breathtaking building lies to the east. It's not as tall as the cathedral but is enormously wide, spanning the entire east side of the colossal plaza. That's where I need to go. That's where the president must be, where my father must be. That's the Palacio Nacional.

Chapter Forty-Seven

I enter the stone plaza from the west side. I check my watch as I walk past the giant flagpole proudly displaying the Mexican flag smack dab in the middle of the plaza. It's *exactly* 12:17 p.m., meaning I have *exactly* two hours to find my dad, get the scabbard in his hand, and save his life.

I walk right up to the grand entrance of the National Palace but there I'm stopped. A man in military uniform carrying an automatic rifle, one of many guarding the entrance, holds out his hand as a gesture that I can't go any further.

"Can't go through here, buddy," he says, eyes constantly scanning the plaza ahead.

"I need to see my dad," I say. "He's a Secret Serviceman. It's really important."

The guard doesn't even bother to look at me. He's still staring off at the people walking throughout the plaza when he says, "I don't care if your father is the president of Russia. You ain't gettin' through."

I start to say something, but stop. This man is clearly

an American doing his job of securing the area surrounding the President of the United States. What can I say to convince this guy to let me in? Nothing. He's under orders and he's going to follow them. And if I make a run for it, I'll just be tackled and arrested, or worse, shot. Either way, I won't be able to save my dad.

So I just walk away from the entrance of the palace and sit down in the plaza next to some tourists. I have to come up with a plan to get in and find Dad and I have less than two hours to do so. *He* has less than two hours to live.

I study the palace to see if there are any other entrances, but everything's heavily guarded, of course. Being displayed on the roof of the palace are flags from all over the world. Must be the countries that are at the summit. What did the man on the street say? Peace Summit. Huh, bet *that's* going well.

I look around the plaza to see if there's anything that can help me. There are just tourists and reporters, tons of them, walking around idly without a care in the world. Snapping a photo here and there, having a snack. Maybe I can pretend to be a reporter to get in. Snag someone's badge and walk right in. But no, they have better security than that. I'll get caught, thrown in a cell, questioned, and my time will run out. So what then? How can I get in?

I stand up and start walking toward the cathedral, hoping for some divine inspiration.

The inside of the cathedral is just as glorious as the outside—the exquisitely carved columns rise hundreds of feet to support a beautifully domed ceiling and the altar looks to be made of solid gold. The Catholics sure do know how to build a church.

I find a quiet place near the altar away from the other

people who've come in to pray or just look around. I get on my knees. I don't normally do this, I don't know quite how to start, so I just begin with what I've seen in the movies.

I fold my hands together, close my eyes, and say, "Lord, God, I'm in need of help. You see, my dad's in trouble and I'm the only one who can save him. I know he's been tough on me, but he's a good man. I know he loves me. I'm not even his real son, just a foster child, but he takes care of me like I'm one of his own. Please, please, send me some advice or help or whatever you can. I can't fail now. I've come so far. He doesn't deserve to die. Not now. Not like this. Please, help me."

I pause, trying to figure out if I'm doing this right and if there's anything else I need to say, but before I can pray any more, a voice speaks up quietly from behind me.

"Ask and ye shall receive."

I spin around on my knees. Standing behind me, well, in front of me now, is a squat little man in an old friar's robe. He's pudgy, almost entirely bald, and hunched over uncomfortably. He's an odd-looking man, but I'd recognize those twinkling eyes anywhere.

"Merlin! Thanks for coming! I need your help!" I say, jumping to my feet.

"Darn! My disguises aren't working so well any more, eh? Oh well. It's still fun to assume another identity for a bit," he says, taking my arm in his.

We begin to walk, very, very slowly, around the cathedral.

"You know, I've always liked churches. Very peaceful. Great place to think, to meditate," he says.

"And to pray," I add.

"Of course."

"So, what's the plan? How are you going to get me into the palace to find my dad? Give me a disguise like the one you have on?"

"Oh, no, I can't do that. I have been able to help you up to this point, sure, but now you must complete the endeavor on your own. It is your charge, your duty. You are the King and it is your scabbard that has the power to protect, not mine."

I'm stunned. No help? Then why is Merlin even here?

"But I can't even get to my father without your help. There's no way! The security's too tight. You've got to help me!" I plead.

"My boy, this is not the most difficult quest you will be faced with, it is merely the first. It is always the task at hand that seems the most treacherous, even when it is not always so. Remember that," Merlin says stoically.

"But this is a matter of life and death! What could be more treacherous than that?"

Merlin stops walking and looks up at the altar.

"Oh, I can think of at least one thing."

And in my heart I know he's right. Life isn't everything. But still, if there's something, *anything*, I can do to save my dad, I'm going to do it.

"Isn't there anything you can do to help?" I ask.

Merlin smiles, his eyes sparkling.

"Well, I suppose a little information couldn't hurt. The word is that the president is to address the world with some big news at 2 p.m., right from the Zócalo. Perhaps then would be a good time to approach your father."

"2 p.m.? That's cutting it a little close, wouldn't you say?" The scabbard must be in my father's hand at exactly 2:17 p.m. in order to save his life, after all.

"Oh, not at all, not at all. There's no such thing as a close call if it is in the hands of fate. If it is destined to be, so shall it be."

I let out a deep breath. I'm not so sure about this. It doesn't seem like much of a plan, but what else can I do? Merlin hasn't steered me wrong yet.

"All right," I say. "And what do I do until then?"

"Well, exactly what you were doing before, I suppose," Merlin suggests.

"What? Praying? I thought you believed in fate and destiny. How is praying going to help?"

Merlin just shrugs and kneels down before the altar, clasping his hands and bowing his head.

"It couldn't hurt."

So I follow suit and begin to pray as well. Merlin and I kneel side by side for almost two hours, silently praying for everything to go well, for my father to be saved.

"I believe it is time," Merlin says, standing up solemnly.

I get up slowly, too. My knees hurt and my legs feel like gelatin, but to be honest, I really haven't felt better in my entire life. I have a great sense of calm, of tranquility, of rejuvenation. I feel ready for whatever lies ahead.

"All right. Are you coming, too?" I ask.

"I will be watching," Merlin says.

"Okay. Thanks. Thanks for everything."

I wrap my arms around him and give him a long, long hug.

"You will make a great king," he says quietly.

"Thanks."

I walk out of the cathedral and back into the plaza where I hope my prayers will be answered.

Chapter Forty-Eight

The whole plaza is full of people now. It's so ridiculously crowded that I can barely move.

I check my watch. It's exactly 2 p.m. There's a platform in front of the cathedral surrounded by reporters facing away from me and into the plaza. This must be from where the president's going to address the enormous crowd.

I make my way through the crowd around the right side to the front of the platform. The left side is cordoned off by barricades and armed men wearing different uniforms representing many different countries. They form a corridor leading from the National Palace to the platform. I check the faces of the guards. None of them are Dad.

I check my watch. It's now 2:06 p.m. I thought Merlin said the speech was going to start at 2 p.m.? If it doesn't start soon and if the president doesn't come out, I'll never find Dad in time.

Some music starts. The tune doesn't sound familiar,

but apparently it's very important. All of the guards of various nationalities salute with their rifles and, one at a time, many prestigious looking men—along with a few women—begin to pour out of the National Palace, waving at the reporters, the hundreds of flashing cameras, and the many video cameras that must be reporting the events live to countries all over the world.

The music being played changes with each diplomat who comes out of the palace. The songs must be condensed versions of each country's national anthem.

The procession of world leaders is slow but steady. The men and women take their seats on the platform as they make their way onto the stage one at a time.

It's now 2:10 p.m. Seven minutes until time's up. The alternating music is still playing. Finally, I hear some familiar sounds. I'd recognize the song anywhere—it's *"Hail to the Chief."*

As it begins playing, the President of the United States steps out of the National Palace and starts walking down the corridor of armed guards. Trailing closely behind him is his private security detail of three Secret Servicemen, one of whom is Dad.

I've got to get to him. There's space between each military guard along the corridor, but the fence-like barricade spans the whole distance from the National Palace to the platform. Still, it's a low barricade, low enough that I can call to my father and hand him the scabbard.

I push through the crowd and get next to the fence between two guards just in front of where the President is waving and smiling. Some people behind me are angry that I'm blocking them, but I don't care and they quickly stop fussing, probably afraid to make too big of a scene in front of such heavily-armed servicemen.

I wait until the President passes me by, then call out, "Dad!"

He's scanning the crowd from behind dark sunglasses, getting who-knows-what vital information pumped into his earpiece, but he still picks up my voice and looks at me. He walks purposefully over to me, whispering something into a hidden microphone as he comes.

"Miles? What are you doing here?" he addresses me, face and body void of emotion, though the tone of his voice shows how truly shocked he is at my presence.

"I came to save you, Dad. I don't have time to explain, but you've got to—"

"Stay here. I'll meet up with you after the President's speech," he interrupts before I can say anything else.

"No! Dad, listen! You've got to take this!" I try to show him the scabbard without drawing the attention of any other guards. They might think I'm pulling a weapon and open fire. But my worrying is for naught—Dad's already back in formation, in perfect step behind the President. He would never not fulfill an obligation or ignore a responsibility, and right now his duty is to guard the President. And he'll do it, even if it means ignoring his son and risking his own life.

It's now 2:13 p.m.

The President steps up onto the platform, shaking hands with each and every diplomat on the stage, before taking his place, not on a seat, but at the podium. He's about to start his speech.

It's 2:14 p.m.

I disappear back into the crowd, trying to be as inconspicuous as possible while still getting front and center with the platform.

"Citizens of the world..." the President begins. A hush comes over the crowd as his voice booms across the plaza.

But I hardly take any notice. I'm trying to figure out how to get to Dad—who's on stage about ten feet behind the President—without getting shot.

"A great accomplishment has been achieved today, one that will go down in history, one that you, your children, and many more generations to come will remember and honor."

Thunderous applause rings out from each and every person gathered. Who knows why.

2:15 p.m.

Let's see. If I can just make my way around the right side there, it appears that I can get Dad's attention without alarming anyone else...

"Today, these great leaders of the world have put aside their differences, *we* have put aside *our* difference, our pride, our own ambitions, for the greater good of humanity. Today, the free people of the world are united as we sign this document." Still at the podium, the President holds up a thick, leather-bound folder with an obviously very important sheet of paper inside, "This document, which will bring momentous peace and security to all nations!"

Again, thunderous applause. Everyone must know more about this Peace Summit than I do, but I don't care what they know. I only have one thing on my mind right now...

2:16.

All right, now or never.

"With my signature and the signatures of my fellow delegates, we will issue in a new world of hope and prosperity for all mankind!"

The President uncaps his pen.

I move to the side of the stage closest to Dad.

"He's got a weapon!" someone yells.

They must mean me.

The crowd starts panicking. Screams go up from everywhere, shrieks of fright and horror, but I still move toward Dad, who is now sprinting to cover the President.

I pull myself onto the stage, remove the King's Scabbard from my belt, and extend it out to hand it to Dad, who is now lunging at the President. I'm only feet behind and jump, too.

"Dad!" I yell as I fall, still reaching out with the scabbard.

But I'm too far away to get it to him even with my arm fully extended, so as I fall I toss the scabbard in Dad's direction.

I feel like I'm seeing the events happening before my eyes unfold in slow motion. Dad has jumped onto the President to cover him from danger and both men are falling to the ground. I'm just behind Dad and falling at his feet. The scabbard is flying through the air and is now touching Dad, falling on top of him and the President. I somehow manage to get a glance of my watch even as I continue falling. 2:17 p.m. But over my watch I see something horrid. It wasn't me they were yelling about when someone cried, "he's got a weapon," it was the man on the opposite side of the President, standing on the left side of the stage, handgun drawn, which is now level with him on the elevated stage.

BANG!

The deafening gun blast echoes out.

Everything goes dark.

C.E. Zyburo

Chapter Forty-Nine

Sounds.

Oh, my head hurts. Wow. It hurts *a lot*.

I open my eyes. Blurry light. Okay, it's focusing now. Huh, this looks familiar. Yeah, I'm in my room.

"He's up! He's waking up!"

Gwen?

She appears overhead, looking down on me. She's as beautiful as ever, but much cleaner than last time I saw her. Much more made-up, too.

Baldwin comes into my field of vision, looking down on me as well.

Huh. This all seems oddly familiar. Like when I was unconscious...

"Okay, what happened this time?" I ask in a voice that sounds pretty rough, like it hasn't been used in a while.

"Holy cow! You can talk!" Baldwin exclaims.

Gwen starts crying immediately.

"Yeah—*Cungh! Cungh!*" I cough. "Why shouldn't I?"

My voice is starting to sound better.

"Uh... Um..." Baldwin stalls, staring at his twiddling thumbs.

"Out with it," I say. "I was unconscious before, you know."

"Yeah, but before you weren't shot in the head!" Baldwin says, then quickly covers his mouth, ashamed at having let the news slip.

"Shot? In the head?" I ask rhetorically, moving my arm up to feel my head. There's an IV attached to my hand and the tube is getting in my way, but I can feel that my head's all bandaged up.

"Yeah, I can't believe it either. Thank God you're okay!" I hear Kay's voice say.

I turn slightly to my right and see him standing at my bedside. Behind him are Mom and Dad, sleeping, basically on top of each other, on a tiny cot in the corner of my room.

Kay sees that I'm looking at them and explains, "They never left your side. Dad was with you all the way back from Mexico and Mom hasn't gone anywhere since you got home. They've been up for almost two days straight, watching you every second. Should I wake them?"

"No, let them sleep," I say. "So that's how long I've been out? Two days again?"

Kay shakes his head.

"Nah, that's how long you've been home. Doctors thought being in a familiar environment might help you recover. You were in the hospital for five days before that."

A week? How the heck have I been knocked out for a whole week?

C.E. Zyburo

"It was a medically induced coma," comes the explanation from a voice to my left. I turn to face him, but I already know who it is. Merlin.

"Quite beyond my capabilities, let me tell you," he continues, "but thank God for it!"

"Hey, if it wasn't for you, old man, he'd probably be dead," says Kay.

Merlin just waves his hand and blushes.

"What do you mean? And how do you know?" I manage to ask. All of this is a lot of information for my pounding head to take in right now.

Baldwin jumps in excitedly with the explanation.

"It's all over the news! You're famous, Miles! You're the kid who saved the President! They have video of everything! Everyone all over the entire world has seen the footage of the bullet somehow going straight through your Dad and the President without hurting them a bit and then hitting you right in the head!"

"Ungh..." I groan. The memory of it, which all comes back in an instant, makes my head hurt tremendously. The right side of my temple just above my ear is in complete anguish.

Gwen punches Baldwin in the arm for having caused me pain.

"Ow! What was that for?" he cries, then, looking at me, "Oh, uh, sorry. Didn't mean to bring up bad memories...but anyway, Merlin was right there to take the shooter down before he could fire any more shots, and then he went straight over to you and performed first aid until the paramedics took over. Here, wanna see?"

Baldwin takes out a new phone and starts to pull up the video.

"Maybe later," I say, turning away. I definitely don't feel up to watching myself get shot in the head right now.

Gwen punches Baldwin again. He stifles his yelp and rubs his arm gingerly.

"Some friends you got here," Kay says, eyeing Baldwin in particular. "An interesting group, to say the least... So anyway, you were treated quickly at the best hospital in Mexico City, but of course, we have the best neurosurgeons here in America, so the President himself had you transported to Johns Hopkins for treatment. Doc said he wasn't sure that he could promise us anything, so I told him to shut it, that you're an Ector and a warrior and would pull through! And look at you! You're fine!" Kay pulls back his arm to slug me playfully, then realizes he probably shouldn't and instead awkwardly pats me on the shoulder.

"What about Ban and Bors? And Grace and her father?" I ask.

"Who?" Kay responds.

"Oh, yeah! That's a whole 'nother story," Baldwin says. "Apparently our cover to go to Wyoming for the week fell apart pretty quickly. There were Amber Alerts out for you, me, and Gwen the day after we left!"

"I tried to cover for you, bro," Kay says, "But everyone got worried pretty quickly when they discovered there was no class trip to Boston."

"Well, thanks for trying," I say.

"So, yeah," Baldwin continues eagerly, "*tons* of people were looking for us, but we didn't even know it. So, since we weren't trying to hide on the way home, we got picked up by the police at the first town we walked into!"

"So Grace and her father and Ban and Bors..." I say, jogging Baldwin's memory which is apparently worse than mine even though *I'm* the one who got shot in the head.

"Oh, yeah! Well Grace and her father are fine. They stayed at their house and we didn't tell anyone about them in case the cops tried to say they kidnapped us or something. And when we left their cottage, Ban and Bors went in the opposite direction of Gwen and I. Said they had pressing matters at home but that we'd all meet up again soon."

Merlin chuckles and says, "Yes, that certainly is true."

"So are we in trouble then? For running away? For wasting the police's time or something?" I ask.

Kay laughs.

"In trouble? Are you kidding me? I don't think you realize what's going on! You saved the *President*! The President of the United States of America! And what's more, you saved the Peace Summit! If the President had been killed the whole thing would have fallen apart, but you saved it! My little brother, the kid with the dragon! Oh, yeah, you better believe they got that on video, too. What were you thinking flying behind a bar, a *bar*, on a dragon? Of course they have security cameras! Oh, and next to a plane? Yeah, real sneaky, real smart, Miles! Anyway, you'll have to tell me all those stories later. But just think of it. My little bro, the savior of the world! My little brother, King Arthur!" Kay exclaims proudly, his whole demeanor more joyous than I have ever seen.

With his boisterous speech, Mom and Dad wake up. They rush over to my bed.

"Oh, Miles! You're awake! Do you feel all right?" Mom asks, tears in her eyes.

"Fine, Ma. My head hurts pretty bad, is all."

"I should say so!" Dad starts with a chuckle. Then, much more seriously, he kneels down by my bed and says, "Listen, son, I... I should have listened to you. I should have—"

"It's all right, Dad," I say. "We're all alive. That's all that matters."

"I love you, Son," Dad says, kissing me gently on the forehead.

"I love you too, Dad. I love you too, Mom. I love you all," I say, tears streaming down my face.

Chapter Fifty

"Are you hungry? Thirsty? What can I get for you?" Gwen asks. Dad and Mom have gone to their room to get some much needed sleep. I'm so glad we're all back together and safe at home.

"I'm fine. Just lay here with me," I say, scooting over to make room for Gwen. She lies down, her body fitting perfectly next to mine.

Merlin is entertaining Baldwin and Kay on the other side of my room with some of his "parlor tricks." Archimedes is happily eating his favorite food, Vietnamese crickets, in his terrarium. The Quest for the King's Scabbard is complete. I couldn't be happier.

Out of the blue my bedroom door is flung open. It's Felicia. She's huffing and puffing like she just ran the Boston Marathon.

"Oh, Mr. Arthur! Thank God you are okay!" She crosses herself, ever the good religious woman. She comes over and grabs my hand and kisses it. "It was a miracle what you did and a miracle that you are alive! God has blessed you!"

"Thanks, Felicia," I say with a smile. She's a lovely woman.

She looks at Gwen lying next to me and blushes.

"Oh, oh! I'm sorry! So sorry! I will leave you alone!" She backs away quickly to the door.

I laugh. "Felicia, it's okay. You can stay if you want."

"Oh, no, no. I have so much to do! Oh, which reminds me! What do you want me to do with all of your mail and what should I tell your visitors?"

"What mail? What visitors?" I ask.

"We were going to let you rest a while before we bothered you about that," Gwen says.

"Oh, sorry! So sorry!" Felicia apologizes.

"No, it's okay," I say, sitting up in my bed for the first time. "My strength's coming back already. What's going on?"

"You have so much mail, Mr. Arthur! It's taking up nearly half of the parlor! And the *people*, ay Dios mío!" Felicia exclaims, crossing herself in exasperation this time.

Merlin comes over to me with Archimedes in one hand and Excalibur sheathed in the King's Scabbard in the other.

"If you are up for it, my King, I think it is time," he says proudly, his eyes twinkling brighter than ever, like galaxies revolving in happy spirals.

"Time for what?" I ask, getting out of bed to test my strength. I can stand, but I'm a bit wobbly. Gwen and Merlin support me on either side.

"For your coronation," Merlin says.

My friends quickly get to work, as if this, whatever it is, has all been planned out. Baldwin helps me get out of my hospital gown and into some nicer clothes while everyone else works to make themselves more presentable as well.

After I'm dressed in my nicest set of clothes, Gwen and Baldwin drape a beautiful red cloak over my shoulders that flows down to my feet and is bordered with exquisitely ornate gold and silver lining of fantastic, elegant design.

"Your parents ordered the finest material for us. Baldwin and I stitched the lining, with Felicia's help and support, of course," Gwen says.

I'm at a loss for words.

Once everyone is spiffed up, we head out.

Gwen and Merlin each grab an arm to help me out of my bedroom and down the elevator. We walk slowly out of the front door, Baldwin pushing my IV stand next to me, Kay carrying Excalibur and Archimedes with Mom and Dad by his side, Felicia following a few steps behind, praying quietly in Spanish.

The fresh air's rejuvenating. It feels great to be outdoors after spending a week cooped up inside, even if I was in a coma for most of it.

"What *exactly* are we doing?" I ask, but my eyes and ears answer the question. At the front gate to our estate is a mass of people, even more people than there were at the plaza in Mexico City. There are reporters, too, hundreds of them, all with cameras rolling. There are people as far as the eye can see, people of all races and ages. Some are crying, some smiling, some holding their arms through the iron-barred fence surrounding my house, reaching out in my direction. As soon as the people in front spot me, they start cheering, and the exuberance spreads through the crowd of people, stretching back and back, over the hills and beyond.

I look around in awe.

"All these people…" I start to say.

"Yes, all these people are here for you," says Merlin.

He kneels before me. The rest of my friends follow suit. Suddenly, the crowd becomes silent. The people in front are the first to kneel and, like the wave of joy that spread through the crowd before, the people all begin to kneel. Even the reporters are on their knees, respecting the will of the people.

Everything's quiet. All eyes, hundreds of thousands of eyes, are on me. I'm the only one standing.

Baldwin steps up and hands me a gorgeous shield of the darkest, burning red imaginable.

"Dragon scales apparently make excellent shields. Ban and Bors added the enarmes themselves," Baldwin says, showing me the strong, leather straps at the back.

I take up the shield. It feels perfect, like it was made just for me. I feel invincible just holding it.

Baldwin bows and returns back to his kneeling position of reverence.

Now Gwen steps up, holding a magnificent, glistening crown of the brightest material I've ever beheld.

I don't know what it can possibly be made of. It's not gold or silver, but rather some odd iridescent substance that's somehow so familiar…

"Forged from the crystals of the Lady's enchanted lake. Grace's father said it will bring great health and longevity to the wearer. Grace even blessed it with the water from the Lake."

C.E. Zyburo

The spherical crystal pebbles have somehow been stretched into thin cords appearing as the most stunning blown glass, all intertwined like twigs in a bird's nest, in a circle forming the base of the crown. All along the circular base, protruding up from the crystal cords, are crosses decorating the top in the most noble fashion. The whole thing seems to act like a prism—despite the crown's clear appearance, it reflects the sunlight in a dazzling display of soft yet brilliant color.

I smile, remembering my dear friends, as Gwen gently places the radiant crown atop my head and resumes her place kneeling at my side.

Finally, Merlin takes Excalibur in the King's Scabbard from Kay and holds the hilt toward me, keeping his head bowed.

I pull Excalibur from the scabbard and hold up the glistening blade. Royal wardrobe, dragon-scale shield, mystical crown, and Excalibur with its miraculous scabbard—I truly feel like a king.

Merlin jumps to his feet and faces the crowd.

"All hail King Arthur!"

All at once, every single person in the entire gathering stands up simultaneously and yells, "All hail King Arthur!" and lets out such a roaring cheer, a cheer even louder than before, a joyous cheer more powerful and loving than any I have ever heard before.

I can't say a thing. I'm so overjoyed.

Gwen is standing next to me. I grab her hand and squeeze it tight.

It's the most amazing feeling in the world. I'm the luckiest person in the world—standing here, having completed my quest and saved my father, covered in precious gifts, surrounded by family and friends, and being cheered by thousands of adoring people. I can hardly believe that it all happened, that it's all *happening*, that any of this is even real.

Merlin smiles, his eyes sparkling as brightly as mine must be.

"So begins the reign of King Arthur."

About the Author

C.E. Zyburo, though he loves to read and write, is probably better known as "Mr. Z" as he is a middle school teacher in Hillsborough County, Florida. He started writing his own stories at a young age and always has a pen and paper close by. He enjoys his rare moments of success on the golf course and hopes to take up fishing and many more adventurous activities once his two young children get a bit older!

CPSIA information can be obtained at www.ICGtesting.com
Printed in the USA
LVOW08s1023121215

465918LV00001B/1/P